Praise for *The Haunting of the Irish Girl*

The twins are back, and off to Ireland to investigate another haunting. The 13-year-olds, Aimée and Juliette, with special psychic abilities, reassemble their team of sleuths, along with a familiar cast and new faces. The story features, without spoilers, the paranormal, a vortex for time travel, magic, auras, ghosts, and "mind-speak." *The Haunting of the Irish Girl's* a fun read, a sort of mix of Nancy Drew and Harry Potter, written in a style reminiscent of Betsy Haynes.
Kevin St. Jarre, author of *Celestine*

The Crystal Chain
"Judi knows how to move a story forward."
Maureen Egan, Author of *The Light from Here*

The Reluctant Ghost of Brivalle Castle
"An imaginative, time-hopping, magical mystery."
Loraine Murray, Youth Services Librarian
Camden Public Library

Also by Judi Valentine

The Crystal Chain

The Reluctant Ghost of Brivalle Castle

The Haunting of the Irish Girl

The Haunting of the Irish Girl
© Judi Valentine, 2021
ISBN: 978-1-7923-2282-2

Quill Hill Publishing
29 Beaver Pond Road
Brunswick, ME 04011
jvalentinebooks@aol.com

Cover Art: FrinaArt Book Cover Designs
Interior Illustrations: Maury Kettell
Stone House and Maps: Public Domain
Inn: Pixabay/Iceberg 90

The Haunting of the Irish Girl

By Judi Valentine

Introduction

We first met twin sisters Aimée and Juliette in my book, *The Crystal Chain*. It became clear these two adventure seekers weren't finished exploring the supernatural. No sooner had they (barely) recovered from their search inside a treacherous, abandoned crystal mine when they learned they were being sent to boarding school for their own protection. However, being Aimée and Juliette, they soon found themselves embroiled in a new mystery, compelled to search for clues to explain a schoolmate's persistent, hovering ghost. In this story, the sisters are once again called to action to help a girl from the wild shores of western Ireland solve the mystery of her brother's treacherous death.

Author's Note

Einstein discovered that time is a field through which we move. Depending on the speed of our movement, time can seem to go faster or slower. Picture two trains moving at different speeds. If we sit in the faster train, the slower one appears to be moving backwards—time slowing down.

Time theorists tell us the past, present, and future happen all at once, and we may view those dimensions from wherever we sit on our own timeline of movement. If we were able to go back in time, we could watch events that occurred then. If we were to go ahead in time, we'd see events of the future. One could say that time, being relative, exists in the eye of the beholder.

I love Einstein's theory of relativity because it offers endless possibilities for time travel adventure stories. I hope you enjoy this one.

Table of Contents

The Haunting of the Irish Girl

Chapter 1

Home

It was great to be back home in the twenty-first century, felt twins Aimée and Juliette, home from their boarding school, the Abbey. The Abbey was an unconventional school, some might even say bizarre. For example, in order to get home, their bodies had to careen through a timeline vortex across four hundred years, to their own century where the school didn't exist at all. Yet, if you lived in seventeenth-century France and looked up a certain hill through an iron gate, you would see a massive stone monastery, with horses and riders trotting from stables to trails, and women in long tunics and colorful head scarves working substantial gardens.

Even more inexplicable was that this seventeenth-century abbey was run by a secret sisterhood with mystical powers. Only students with sixth sense abilities were allowed in, and every girl had to be recommended by a sorceress. And really, how many sorceresses does anyone know?

The twins' schoolmate Lil had traveled home with them for the holiday. Lil hadn't experienced a family Christmas since she was five. Her mother had abandoned the family soon after, and her father had shunted her off to the Abbey, making it a point to be away on business, holiday or not.

It was amazing the twins were friends at all with Lil. Until last semester, she'd been the school's mean girl. After her extremely bad judgment had nearly gotten someone killed, she had admitted her mistake, repented, and reformed. Although not in every way, as you'll discover.

Now, as the girls craned their necks to admire the inn's enormously tall Christmas tree, a teenage boy sprang into the room waving a sheet of paper. It was Danni, the twins' adopted brother. Danni's parents had died when he was a baby.

Afterward, he'd lived with his grandfather, a retired train conductor who spent more time with his wine bottles than with him. Eventually, the ill-tempered man died. The sisters soon learned that their best summer pal was headed to an orphanage. What a relief when their parents realized Danni was living alone on sardines and eggs and had agreed to take him in.

Aimée turned away from the rocket-shaped fir tree and called out to her new brother, "Danni, your socks! One's blue and one's brown!" She glared at his shirt hanging half in and half out of wrinkled pants. One sleeve was rolled up and the other neatly buttoned at the wrist.

Danni looked down. "These were closest when I got dressed."

Although no longer an orphan, habits from living at the bleak railway cottage remained with him. Wavy brown hair flipped around every which way as if never having met a brush. And he hated mirrors, so never looked one in the eye.

A typical sister, Aimée moved in to straighten his shirt when he put up a hand. "Wait! I have an important message from the manor house. Charlotte is on her way." He grinned, showing a space between his top teeth, which gave his letter S a slight splutter.

"I finally get to meet the last member of your detective team." Danni offered Lil a tiny grin. His cheeks pinked up. He wasn't used to being around so many girls.

Aimée seized the note, hand-written on formal paper. It was from Charlotte's mother, a real duchess. Aimée read out loud:

We are pleased to inform you Charlotte will arrive at the inn by late afternoon on Sunday, accepting your kind invitation to stay to the end of the holiday.

Regards,

Madame Mirabelle,

Brivalle Castle Manor

Lil clapped her hands. "Our team will be together again."

The team consisted of twins Aimée and Juliette, Lil, and Charlotte. Together, they'd already solved one supernatural mystery.

"Sunday! That's today!" Aimée shouted as her phone pinged.

On my way. Maman approved.

"Charlotte's on her way now!" Aimée exclaimed. She couldn't wait to introduce Charlotte to every-one where she and her sister had lived since babyhood. The inn, Auberge des Étoiles, was a refurbished chateau on the edge of a tiny French village. Today the place was bustling with families staying for the holiday.

"When do we talk about Kalin?" Danni asked, feeling impatient. "Remember the Irish girl I wrote about, here with her parents? We have to help her. I think she might die if we don't."

"That sounds a bit dramatic," Lil said. "But, yeah, tell us right now."

Danni blushed. He wasn't used to girls being so direct. On the other hand, there was Aimée. His nose went up as he sniffed the air. "Wait. Chef Marie just took croissants out of the oven. Let's go while they're hot." Eating was Danni's favorite activity.

Taking in the yeasty smells of baking, they hurried down the central hall to the chef's domain with oversized windows overlooking frosty herb gardens. Marie bustled about under a cloud of flour as she prepared tonight's dessert for twenty guests.

Marie was from Joyeux and had worked at the inn since the twins' parents bought it ten years before. She'd known the girls since they were toddlers and missed them terribly while they were away at school. When at home, she could keep an eye on their escapades. Now she had no idea what they were up to, except to know it would be edged with danger.

Chef Marie glanced up, and seeing the girls and Danni in the doorway, her face brightened. Struggling with English she said, "Come, come, *vous devez tous manger*, you must all eat some." She wiped her hands on her apron, picked up a tray, and covered it with a starched white cloth. Then she added croissants, flaky and warm, and a crock of strawberry jam.

Danni hustled over and took the tray. He set it down on a long wooden table before a row of multi-glass-paned windows glistening with sunshine. As he slid onto the bench next to Lil, his stomach growled as if a tiger lived inside.

Aimée and Juliette giggled fondly. As usual Danni was hungry. At the end of summer, he'd come to the inn all skin and bones. Now he looked more like a normal sixteen-year-old.

Aimée said in French, "Marie, our schoolmate Charlotte will be here today. She's part of our first-rate detective team, with Lil, here."

The girls worked well as a team, even with their age differences. The twins were thirteen, Charlotte fifteen, and Lil, at sixteen, was practically an adult. At least she thought so.

At the words *detective team*, Marie's face clouded up as she poured steaming chocolate into four mugs. She topped each one with fresh whipped cream, sprinkled with cinnamon. "You look for trouble, Aimée?" The chef was one of the few people who could tell the twins apart. Aimée had a brown mark under her left eye, shaped like a small pair of wings.

"Don't worry," Aimée assured her. "We know what we're doing this time, right, Juliette?" Her sister nodded, but not as emphatically as Aimée had hoped.

Taking on the mannerisms of a butler, Danni handed a spicy scented beverage to each girl, flushing again as he saw Lil watching him.

She nodded her thanks with a tiny smile and said, "Tell us about Kalin."

Danni sat down next to her and swallowed a big gulp of hot chocolate, leaving a milky mustache on his lip. He looked around for eavesdropping guests, then whispered, "She's here from Ireland with her parents. I haven't heard her say a single word, and she never looks anyone in the eye. It's like she's living on a different planet."

The girls exchanged glances.

"Have you tried talking to her?" Lil asked.

"I don't think she can be reached. Once, when I was on the back stairs, I heard her parents say the word *trauma*. I think something bad happened to her back in Ireland."

"What else do you know?" Aimée asked.

"Aunt Celeste says she just turned thirteen, like you, but she looks younger. She's practically as thin as Grandpère's walking stick, hardly eats, and mostly stays in her room or in the library staring out the window. One day she went into the woods, and I followed her. After a while she stretched out on some pine needles and stared straight up, as if ..."

"... as if in a trance?" Lil interrupted. Not another ghost possession, she thought.

"More like tuned out," he said. "I hid, but she didn't seem to know I was there."

"You didn't leave her alone?" Juliette asked, as much of a worrier as Chef Marie.

"Of course not. After a while she walked back. I shadowed her from a distance."

Juliette set down her mug. "Where is she now? I could look at her aura for clues."

Danni's eyebrows shot up. "Remind me about this aura thing." He knew the girls had special abilities, but it was confusing. He hadn't had many friends growing up at the train station, never mind friends with super abilities.

Juliette said, "Remember when I saw those murky colors around your grandfather? Each person has energy around their body, invisible to most people. The colors can tell us things."

Danni jumped up. "Let's go now. We need clues about Kalin's trauma."

Chapter 2

Kalin's Mystery

Juliette and Danni slipped into the library and closed the door. Kalin sat on the window seat staring out the window, her thin legs stretched out.

"Hi," Juliette said, offering a little wave as she walked over to a nearby bookshelf. She pulled out a favorite, *A Wrinkle in Time*, and sat before the fire. Danni grabbed his open copy of *The Hitchhiker's Guide to the Galaxy* and dropped into the chair next to Juliette, who moved hers slightly for a better view of Kalin.

The thin girl wore a purple scarf banded around short, red hair that stuck out erratically. High cheekbones protruded from a pale face. Her gaze didn't waver as the two moved around in the library, as if she didn't even see them.

She looks so sad, thought Juliette, her own heart melting. Softening her gaze, she took in the space around Kalin's body. At first, she saw no auric colors at all. Then shades of brown appeared with fragments of black swirling around in a mournful pattern. The color field was rimmed in gray, which Juliette knew to be fear, deeply entrenched fear. She also knew that black meant grief. She'd never seen an aura so sorrowful. Whatever happened to Kalin had not only terrified her, it had broken her heart.

Juliette and Danni read for a while, and after a hidden prompt for Danni to leave, Juliette approached. "Hi there, I'm Juliette. Would you join me sometime for hot chocolate?"

Kalin turned to her and, as their eyes met, Juliette felt a jolt of deep anguish. The wave nearly pushed her back. As the sensation melted away, Juliette looked into deep, green eyes that reminded her of the forbidden forest at the Abbey. She shivered, remembering the primitive woodland teaming with wild animals and thick vines.

Kalin pondered the invitation. Then she nodded ever so slightly, slid off the window seat, and left the room without a word.

Juliette let out a breath. Well, it's a start, she thought, and turned to climb the stairs to her room. Danni and Aimée intercepted her on the way. "How did it go?" Danni asked.

Juliette described the limited exchange. "At least she agreed to meet."

"Kalin's lucky to be here while you're all together," Danni said. "You guys helped Charlotte release her ghost. I think you can help Kalin, too."

Danni was talking about how the girls had freed the phantom ancestor that had haunted Charlotte for ten long years, nearly ruining her life.

You'll hear more about Charlotte's ghost, but for now let's worry with Juliette.

Juliette shook her head somberly. "Let's get real. We can't solve Kalin's mystery in two weeks. Then we're back at school."

"School's exactly what I was thinking," Danni said. "Maybe your parents can tell Kalin's parents about the Abbey. Your detective team could figure things out while you're all there."

Juliette pulled her silvery blond side braid, a nervous habit. Aimée's identical braid never looked as neat as her sister's.

Danni pushed, "Kalin should go to school with you. You have the sisterhood and that wizard. Couldn't they help?"

Aimée jumped in. "Danni's right. I think being at the Abbey would help. She agreed to meet you, right? Tell her about the school then."

Danni's eyes brightened at having an ally. "It can't hurt to tell her. Then our parents could talk to her parents. And Charlotte could tell them how the school helped her."

Juliette touched his arm. "You really care about her, don't you, Danni?"

"I can tell she's given up. I know what that's like. When Grandpère died, your family saved me from going to an orphanage." Living alone in a barely furnished depot building was no proper home for a boy.

Danni raised his chin. "She'll be safe at school. You can work on the mystery there."

"Maybe," Juliette said. Things were getting way too complicated. She couldn't abide another troublesome semester at school.

As they climbed the stairs, Aimée's more confident mind churned ideas around. First, Kalin would need a referral. No one got into the Abbey without one. Their neighbor, Madame Villars, was a member of the same secret sisterhood that ran the school. They'd have to get one from her. Then convince Kalin and her parents. Once at school, solving the mystery might be hard, but the team was good at mysteries. At least they had been once. For Charlotte's ghost.

Danni broke into her thoughts. "I wish I could go to that school with you. I could help."

"I wish you could too, Danni, but you'd stick horribly out as a boy. Keep writing to us."

Danni glanced down the hall and remembered the towels. "Gotta go. Chores to finish."

On his way to the laundry room, Danni thought he wanted to do more than write letters. He felt safe at the inn and loved his new parents, but if he didn't have an adventure of his own soon, he'd die of boredom.

We'll just have to wait and see what he does about that.

Chapter 3

Charlotte Arrives

Juliette pulled her sister toward their quaint little attic room on the fourth floor. She needed to talk before Charlotte arrived, and before everyone got too excited about Kalin's mystery.

"What's the matter?" Aimée asked, closing the door.

Juliette worried her braid. "How can we help Kalin? What if we don't have the right gifts?"

"We do," Aimée argued. "Freeing Charlotte's ghost was hard, but we did it."

Juliette clung to her plait as if it were a life vest. "We were nearly poisoned and mauled by a wolf!" She pictured the she-wolf's teeth as it growled protecting her babies.

"True. But it came out all right in the end. Charlotte's okay now, isn't she?"

Juliette plopped down on her bright yellow bean bag. "All I'm saying is Kalin's mystery seems more serious than Charlotte's. What if we make things worse?"

Aimée walked to the window and stared out. She appreciated her sister's caution, she really did. Her own tendency was to rush in. "Okay, I get it. I'll try not to be so pushy. Until we know more ... for now."

Juliette's eyebrows rose. "Promise?" she asked.

Aimée nodded and pulled her sister up. "Let's go check on Lil. She always cheers us up."

~

Aimée knocked on Lil's guestroom door just as Danni appeared behind them, having finished folding the morning's linens. "Just in time," she said.

"Come in!" Lil said, and turned away from the window where she'd sat, spying out at the world. "How did it go with Kalin? Whoa!" she said, jumping off the seat. "Fill me in later. The limo ... it's here! Charlotte is here!"

Everyone raced for the bedroom doorway at the same time, crushing Lil and Danni together inside the opening. His head was close to hers, and he closed his eyes inhaling the scent of her hair. He smiled thinking how much he loved lemon.

"Let's go," Aimée said, pushing, and they all popped into the hallway.

Aimée bolted toward the staircase and started down while Lil and Danni recovered from their close encounter.

"Sorry," Danni said, his face heating up. Then, regaining a sense of dignity, he swung an arm toward the stairs. "Ladies first."

Lil concealed a grin, and as she hurried to catch the twins, her heart pummeled her chest. She couldn't tell if it was from being so close to Danni or because she'd be seeing Charlotte within minutes. Danni's footsteps sounded behind her as they all ran out onto the circular driveway.

The big black limousine crept under the portico with Aimée jogging alongside. Charlotte waved excitedly from the back seat. The chauffeur, Gustav, shed his formal bearing with a chuckle. He'd known Charlotte for many years, and she'd never had friends like this. The car had barely slowed when she tumbled out and into the arms of the waiting sisters.

Lil joined them in a loud celebration but glanced back to notice Danni had put his hands over his ears. Our behavior must look juvenile to him, she thought, stepping back. "Ladies. Let's get Charlotte settled in," she said, more adult-like. After all, she was sixteen.

Danni walked to the back of the car shaking his head. He realized he had a lot to learn about girls. "I'll help with the luggage," he told Gustav, who had pulled up the trunk.

Aimée cried out, "Wait, Danni! First, you have to meet Charlotte." She gazed at her brother with affection. Even with new clothes, he looked adorably disheveled.

Gustav winked. "You go ahead. I'll take care of this."

Danni froze. He wasn't much for meeting people. When he'd lived with his grandfather in that isolated train depot, visitors were rare. And until he'd met the twins last summer near the crystal mine, he'd had no regular pals. Unless you called his grandfather's wine broker a pal.

"Danni. *Viens ici*, come here!"

Danni shuffled toward the girls but stood back, his heart flapping like a newly caught fish. He liked girls, but so many, and all at once?

Aimée pulled him in to face Charlotte. "This is who we've wanted you to meet. Charlotte, the fourth member of our first-rate detective team."

Charlotte parted rosy lips to show perfect white teeth. "I've wanted to meet you too, Danni," she said, her voice low and rich. "I love the drawings you send. I can tell you like outer space and aliens."

Danni wanted to say something clever. Well, anything really, and be done with it and safely back in the laundry room. But he found himself unable to look away from Charlotte. Those eyes! True emerald green, he thought. Her honey-colored hair was pulled back into a fancy twist. Strands flew around her face, refusing to cooperate. He took in her suede riding skirt, tweed blazer, and riding boots. An antique timepiece hung around her neck. He'd never seen anyone so elegant.

Danni's admiration-trance was interrupted when Aimée shook his arm. "Let's go inside. We want Charlotte to meet Maman." Aimée put an arm through Charlotte's and walked her to the door. "But first let's get you settled in. You're sharing a room with Lil."

After witnessing Danni go all googly, Lil's face that had beamed pure joy over Charlotte's arrival now wore a tight grimace. Not again, she wailed silently, and her stomach sank. She remembered how her first crush, the groomsman at the Abbey, had fallen in love with Charlotte the second he'd met her. Lil was no competition to someone who'd been trained to be a duchess. Slipping away from the little group, she escaped up the stairs. Although her legs felt like two stone pillars, she couldn't get to her room fast enough. It doesn't matter, she told herself as she climbed. I thought Danni and I made a connection, but maybe I imagined it. My imagination does make things up, and then gets me into trouble.

Once in her room, Lil walked to the mirror hanging over her dresser. In stark contrast to jet-black hair and coal-black eyes, a snow-white face stared back. She took in the white streak that ran from her widow's peak to the bottom of her long ponytail—the family mark. The dramatic streak looked better on her father. When she was younger, she'd fearfully believed he was Count Dracula. Maybe that's who she really was, a daughter of Count Dracula.

Giggling, fumbling noises reached her from the staircase, and the door pushed open as the sisters brought in Charlotte and her bags. Danni was not with them.

Lil put on her most convincing happy face. "Charlotte, I thought you'd like the bed under the skylight." Pointing to the smaller bed tucked under the eaves, Lil said, "I prefer that one."

Charlotte laughed. "Leave it to Lil to love dark, possibly haunted spaces."

Lil pulled a serious face. "You never know what forces lurk in the shadows. I don't get spooked easily—as you know."

"We do know," Charlotte said and gave her a tight hug. "Lil, our brave knight."

Lil relaxed and hugged her back.

Charlotte turned slowly, taking in the room's slanted white ceilings and bright skylights. Squares of sunshine rested on flowered bedspreads, and sunlight flickered off mirrors hanging over whimsically stenciled bureaus. Charlotte tapped a set of crystals dangling from a skylight, and the light prisms flickered. "What a cozy room. Your inn looks so unique. I can't wait for a tour."

Aimée said, "Maybe unpack first? Then we'll fill you in on the next mystery."

"What mystery?" Charlotte asked.

"Let's tell her now," Aimée urged. "I can't wait another second."

Juliette gave her sister a concerned look as the four sat, cross-legged on a bed.

Aimée felt her sister pulling on the reins, the downside of being a twin. She took in a breath to slow down, then said, "Juliette, you tell. You talked to Kalin ... sort of."

"We didn't really talk, but I got a teeny sign she might want to. I'm worried though." She paused. "You haven't seen her; she looks sick. Even if she does come to school, I don't think she could sit for classes, or even for meals. Charlotte, at least you joined us in the dining room, even though you couldn't attend classes. I worry she'll end up in the infirmary."

"Wow," Lil said. "She sounds haunted. Who would she room with then?"

The others turned to Lil as if she'd answered her own question.

"Me?" She uttered, unbelieving.

Then everyone started to talk at once.

Juliette put up a hand. "Wait. First, we need to find out what's wrong with her."

Aimée rolled off the bed. "You're right. And since Kalin's not talking, our next step is to visit Madame Villars. Maybe she can figure it out using her sorceress skills. And besides, we haven't seen Zana in an age. I've missed her so much."

"Madame Villars? Zana? Who are they?" Charlotte asked.

The twins looked at each other as if protecting a great secret.

"What have you two been hiding from us?" Charlotte pressed.

Lil crossed her arms. "Yeah, spill it."

Aimée sighed. "It's about the trouble we got into last summer, and why we were sent to the Abbey in the first place. She walked to the door. "We need to go to Madame Villars."

Lil unwrapped her lanky legs and towered over them from her nearly six-foot height. "I am so loving this detective work and dying to meet your sorceress. And we have another mystery to solve." Lil loved solving mysteries, especially if it involved spying and figuring out clues.

Charlotte stayed on the bed. "We just show up? Without an invitation?" She never went to anyone's house without one.

Aimée fluttered her hand. "No invitation needed. She's probably watching us right now through her waterfall."

"Her what?" Lil and Charlotte asked together.

"You'll see," Aimée said mischievously. "Let's go."

Will the twins ever tell the story of what happened last summer? More importantly, would knowing about last summer change what's about to happen?

Chapter 4

The Changeling

The girls searched for Danni to tell him they were headed to Madame Villars', which doubled as a quick tour of the inn. The sisters were touched by Charlotte's immediate love for the restored chateau; they remembered its leaky ceilings and cracked walls when they first moved in.

"How did your parents find this treasure anyway?" Charlotte asked, as they moved in and out of various rooms decorated in the traditional style. Only the game room looked slightly modern with a couple of computers and charging stations. In addition, there was an elaborately carved pool table, a dart board, and tables set up with chess and checkers. The idea was for people to get away from the gadgets and stressors of modern-day life. To relax in the quiet countryside of France.

After nodding at guests sipping coffee in the dining room and visiting the library, they headed for the kitchen. Aimée replied, "When we lived in the U.S., where we were born, my parents wanted to own an inn. But they were all too expensive. Then they saw an ad for a run-down chateau in an old French village with a happy name: Joyeux. We flew here right away and then stayed. My parents refinished most of the inn themselves and have managed it together. That is until Papa got a job. Now he's gone for days at a time as an astronomer at the Geneva Observatory." She smiled, "It's pure coincidence that Danni loves outer space too. He follows Papa around like a puppy whenever he's home."

"You must miss your papa terribly," Charlotte said, looking at two unhappy faces.

"We do," Juliette said. "Maman says we've become too wild."

They found Danni in the kitchen begging Chef Marie for food. Just as he was about to shove a crusty muffin into his mouth, Aimée grabbed his arm.

"No time for that, Danni. We're headed to the olive grove to see Madame Villars."

"But … it's a chocolate center."

"Kidding!" Aimée couldn't get enough of teasing him. "Eat it on the way; we're leaving now." The girls followed her to the back door of the inn.

"Coming," Danni said, spewing a waterfall of crumbs, as he ran to catch up.

~

The girls and Danni walked along the cobblestone drive toward a stand of woods. The hazy sun shone down, but no one felt its winter rays. Halfway down, they veered onto a wide path that led to the woods' edge. Aimée and Danni pushed into the lead with Juliette behind.

Lil and Charlotte followed cautiously, memorizing landmarks in case they became separated. Soon Aimée turned onto a narrow trail edged by tall evergreen trees that forced them into single file. A sudden gust of wind made Lil and Charlotte tighten their scarves. That's when they noticed the humming.

"Does anyone else feel weird?" Lil yelled.

"I do," Charlotte slurred. "My whole body's vibrating, even my mouth."

Aimée turned back. Her voice hummed. "That's just Madame's spell, a kind of electric fence for humans. It won't hurt you."

"How do you know? It feels like it could hurt," Charlotte said.

"No worries. We've felt this a hundred times," Aimée reassured her.

Not reassured at all, their discomfort intensified by the minute. It felt as if they were being invited and repelled at the same time. And what was that shimmery stuff that would suddenly disappear when they stared at it? Were they being watched?

Danni turned onto a carriage trail surrounded by open fields of frozen grass. A variety of animal tracks were molded into the ground. Fascinated, Charlotte bent over to examine them. Her own sixth-sense gift was being able to talk to animals through mind-speak.

She was pulled upright by Lil who urged, "Come on. We have to keep up."

Frost crunched underfoot as the group approached a tall, iron gate sitting in the middle of a tall, thick hedgerow. Everyone stopped. The center of the gate had no keyhole or latch. In its place was a copper plaque with an array of metaphysical carvings: a wizard holding a staff, tarot cards, and crystal balls flickering with real light. In the center of the plaque was the image of a wolfhound sitting like the Sphinx, only it had the face of a girl.

Lil leaned into Charlotte. "This must be the entrance to the sorceress's domain."

"Probably," Charlotte whispered back. "But it's spooking me out." She turned to look at the row of short, thick olive trees. Had they just moved closer? Gaping holes in the trees seemed to cry out a warning. Her body vibrated more intensively now, and the back of her neck buzzed, prickling her spine. Panicked, she spun around ready to run.

"Don't go!" Danni yelled. "That's the whole point, see? It's how Madame V uses magic to keep intruders away." He turned away and tilted his head forward, as if waiting for someone. No sound could be heard except for twigs and branches crackling in the wind. Then he pointed to a four-legged animal in the distance racing toward them, its gait long and graceful. "There she is. There's Zana come to meet us."

"Zana!" The twins yelled. "We've missed you."

A sleek ginger-colored animal came to an abrupt stop before the gate, and sat on its haunches. With eyes the color of molasses, the wolfhound stared unblinking at the plaque. After a few seconds the gate creaked open, splitting the plaque in two.

The creature, released from what seemed to be a spell of some kind, bounded over to Danni and stood up for a hug. The twins joined in, and after a noisy greeting, the hound dropped onto all fours and sat still as a stone again. Its image hazed and blurred, and as Lil and Charlotte stared, eyes as big as saucers, the creature transformed into something completely different—a girl with long, copper-colored hair.

All body vibrations stopped.

Lil stared, unbelieving. "Wait. How...?"

Danni laughed uproariously, his usual shyness disappearing. Coughing to get hold of himself, he said formally, "Lil and Charlotte, I would like you to meet Zana."

Zana offered a bashful smile as she flipped her waist-length hair over her shoulders.

Desiring to get on the good side of this conundrum of a creature, Lil and Charlotte held out a hand. Zana took their hands inside her own two and squeezed gently.

Her elfin ears were the only clue that she wasn't totally human.

Chapter 5

The Sorceress

Zana led the little troupe down the carriage road toward a stone farmhouse sitting in an open clearing some distance away. Stones crumbled here and there from age, but the porch railings had been freshly painted white, giving the house a reassuring, cheery appearance. Harvested gardens and a thick grove of olive trees surrounded the place. What looked like beehives stood on planks near the barn noisy with animals.

As they got closer, Lil and Charlotte kept stealing glances at Zana. Would she morph back into a wolfhound? Or do something else super extraordinary? But no, she acted like any girlfriend catching up on news with the twins.

Aimée kept her entertained with stories of their escapades at the Abbey. How they'd broken the rules—not once but three times—and gone into the forbidden forest, a primordial stew of overgrown foliage where wild animals roamed. Some might think Aimée was making up these extravagant adventures, but Zana listened wide-eyed, believing everything she said.

Lil's long legs caught up with Danni, and she grabbed his arm. "I have a question. Will Madame V have to meet Kalin? That might not be possible, you know."

Danni pictured the mind-bending waterfall. "Won't be a problem. You'll see why."

Waiting on the porch was a small woman looking nothing at all like a sorceress. She wore a green woolen skirt hanging low over black wellies. The skirt was topped by a purple sweater under a loose green vest. The breeze blew black, wavy hair around an unexpectedly pretty face with coffee-colored eyes and thick eyebrows. She grabbed at flyaway hair strands and tucked them into a loose bun at the nape of her neck.

Charlotte whispered to Lil, "She looks completely normal, if a bit old fashioned."

The sorceress held out both arms in welcome. "Hello, hello. How lovely you girls are. I'm Madame

Villars, and you've already met Zana." Her magnetic eyes turned to Danni. "My boy, you must visit more often. You're not so far away. And, sisters, we've missed you too. Zana has especially."

Although they stood back, Lil and Charlotte did not escape Madame's penetrating stare. "Come girls," she said. "We'll share a cup of tea. I think you'll find that I'm sometimes normal." She opened the door and swept everyone inside. Lil and Charlotte exchanged glances, then followed.

Madame led them into her oversized kitchen. The little group had to zig and zag in between huge wooden vats giving off the pungent smell of olives ripening in their juices. A line of tall windows took up an entire wall and overlooked the grove. Slate countertops ran the length of two walls and were set up as a plant workshop. Piles of drying herbs spread about emitted a potpourri of scents—mint, rosehips, lavender. A Bunsen burner stood ready next to a set of antiquated scales. Prisms of color from suspended glass vials danced around the room as sunlight illuminated their contents. Earthy greens, sunset purples, glittering golds.

"Don't mind the hodgepodge," Madame said, her arms sweeping the room. "As the twins know, I make cosmetics for the inn." She pointed to a long, wooden table, "Sit, sit. Pull up chairs. Get comfortable." Water hissed from a heavy black pot that she pulled from the stovetop.

Zana and Danni rushed around dragging wooden chairs around a thick round table standing substantially on a worn carpet of faded reds and browns.

Everyone sat.

Lil heard water flowing and turned to look at the wall behind her. "Look at that. I've never seen an inside waterfall so big, or so..." She stopped, mesmerized by the wide column of water as it gurgled down into a pool at the base. The fountain made a lilting sound like a musical instrument. She turned around to see the sorceress watching her.

"You like the waterfall, Lil? We call her the Maiden of Aran, a name from an old tale."

"Was there a real Maiden of Aran?" Lil asked.

"Yes, in Ireland where our family is originally from. The tale says the maiden fell in with the fairy people. They came to love her as their own and gifted her with this waterfall. For centuries it has been passed down—our family's mirror of truth."

Madame motioned, "Now then, Zana, serve tea, and we'll show our guests what the maiden can do. I understand you want to help a girl named Kalin. The maiden may help us."

Danni jumped up to help Zana place cups, spoons, honey, and steaming milk on the table. Lil watched him closely to see if he paid special attention to Zana. But Danni showed the same deference to all the girls.

Once Zana had poured, Madame pulled her chair closer to the gurgling flow. She raised her arms as if to embrace the waterfall, and then she sang,

"Winter's day, fairies say, what news does the maiden have today?"

A soft mist vaporized from the water's surface and drifted toward the little group, tickling their noses and lips. The very air came alive, whirling and blowing Madame's hair into a nimbus of curls as an image appeared inside the watery flow. Blurry at first, it then sharpened.

Everyone leaned in.

A young man with carrot-red hair rows a heavy wooden skiff along a length of coastline where rocky cliffs rise straight and high above the sea. Waves crash against the beachy lowlands, reaching for rocky heights. The young man paddles toward the beach, then rides the waves to drift in between two massive boulders. As the bow hits sand, he jumps out and turns toward a sound. A boat approaches from some distance. Recognizing the craft, he pulls his skiff behind a boulder and ducks low into several feet of water.

The suspicious boat motors toward an inlet not far away and hits the beach. The pilot shuts down the engine, jumps off, and ties his line to a granite structure sunk deep into the earth. He re-embarks and stares down at three large barrels sitting on his stern. Grunting, he unloads all three, rolling them inside a cave at the back of the flatland to sit with other casks. When finished, he unties the line and jumps onto the boat. Turning, he spies the redheaded man and grins fiendishly, showing a mouth full of crooked, yellow teeth. Pushing off, he climbs aboard and motors away.

The little group held their breath as the vision blurred out. Then a new image appeared.

A fiery explosion fills the sky, followed by flames and plumes of thick smoke. Wooden oars and debris fly high, covering a vivid blue sky with billowing blacks and grays.

Way too soon, the vision turned slurry and evaporated.

Aimée rushed toward the misting fountain. "Wait! There has to be more." But the image was gone, and now only water gushed down the slab, as if nothing horrible had just happened.

Mystified and all talking at once, the group turned toward Madame Villars.

"Is that all we get?" Lil asked.

Madame held up a hand. "Can you hear? The maiden still sings. This means she has more to show."

The misty haze grew thicker again and coalesced into another scene.

Kalin, her flame-red hair unmistakable, sits on a rock staring out to sea. The water is wild with waves that nearly overturn a small boat as it powers in closer.

As the boat approaches the harbor, Kalin runs down the sandy path and hops onto a wooden dock. She runs to the very end, jumping and waving both her arms. Long hair blows around in the wind, and she yells out as if greeting a loved one. Watching the boat edge up to the dock, she seems surprised as a man with an angry face and a mess of tangled hair ties off the boat. He jumps onto the dock and pushes by Kalin, nearly knocking her into the water.

"Where's Finn?" she cries. But the man grins, baring twisted teeth, then hurries up the hill toward the village. She stares out to sea as if resuming her search. In the next instant, she drops to her knees, her mouth forming a silent scream. Her body shakes as if she's seen a most dreadful thing.

Once again, the image disappeared, and the waterfall returned to its natural flowing state. The room had become stone silent. Both images had been almost too terrible to witness. It was clear that something horrible had happened to Kalin, but what? A slew of questions poured into everyone's minds.

Madame Villars turned back to them with a look of regret. "I'm sorry to have upset you, but you must know of the dangers in helping Kalin. The reasons for the explosion run deep, and I invoked these flashbacks to offer clues."

Charlotte fidgeted with her timepiece. "That man in the rowing skiff ... he looks like Kalin. Do you think it was her brother? Maybe this is why she's so traumatized."

Lil stabbed a finger toward the fountain. "I think he was her brother. It looks like he was killed ... by that creepy man."

"Maybe that's why they left Ireland," Danni said. "Maybe he wants to hurt Kalin too."

Charlotte turned to the sorceress. "Do you think going to the Abbey will help her? I was afraid to go, but these girls"—she threw them an affectionate glance—"they solved my haunting."

"The only person who can answer that is Kalin," Madame V said.

Juliette looked at the fountain. "Can you see in there how she'd do at school?"

"The maiden doesn't read the future, dear. But now you know why Kalin suffers."

The room went quiet as everyone's thoughts drilled more deeply into Kalin's mystery.

Juliette spoke. "Kalin seemed okay with meeting. I'll tell her about school then. If she's open to it, our parents could talk to her parents." She was beginning to agree with her sister.

Danni's head bobbed up and down, relieved someone had come up with a next step. He was convinced Kalin was in serious danger. "Madame Villars, if Kalin wants to go to the Abbey, will you recommend her?"

"Oh yes, dear. I agree it's a safer place for her now."

～

No one spoke for a long time on the solemn hike

back to the inn. As the little group broke out of the woods and onto the inn's cobblestone drive, Juliette brought up something the team had been pondering. "Did anyone notice Kalin has the gift of clairvoyance?"

"Clairvoyance? What's that?" Danni asked.

"It's a kind of sixth sense where you see things outside of normal eyesight. Remember when Kalin all of a sudden screamed and cried? I think she'd seen what happened—the explosion, her brother. It was too far away to see with her own eyes."

"It looks that way," Lil said. "I think her brother caught that creepy guy hiding something important in the caves, like the old smuggling days. And to get rid of him, the guy put an explosive in his boat."

"Exactly," Danni said. "Maybe he'd been following the guy. Maybe the guy was stealing stuff." He slapped his head. "Wait. Those barrels. I noticed a stamped logo on them. I'll look it up online as soon as we get back."

"I know one thing," Aimée said somberly. "If I'd seen someone, especially my own family, blown up, I'd be in a zombie trance too."

"And remember," Juliette said, tugging her braid, "Madame V said the reason for the explosion runs deep. If Danni's right and she is in danger, she has to come to school. No one would find her back in 1659. I'm nervous about talking to her, though."

"If anyone can reason with her, you can," Aimée reassured her sister.

"Don't ask me to," Lil said. "I can spy around and figure out clues, but I'm no good at anything requiring diplomacy." The other girls nodded their agreement.

"Think about it," Charlotte said. "Kalin saw the face of the man who hid those casks. Maybe she told her parents, and maybe that's why they brought her all the way to France. To hide her."

"There's definitely something strange going on," Danni agreed. "Kalin doesn't act normal, and her parents don't either. But then, what do I know about normal? I grew up alone in a train station with a boozer."

"Good point," Lil said. "We're all pretty weird in our own way."

No one spoke again as the sky deepened its twilight blue blanket. And as the dazzling full moon inched up the horizon, they each sunk deeper into the murky waters of Kalin's mystery.

Chapter 6

A Date with Kalin

Kalin sat in her usual spot on the window bench of the library. She felt safe here. Tall windows sheltered her on three sides and offered a clear view of the woods and gardens. Her mind focused on nothing in particular. If she were to think, she'd admit to seeing winter-dead trees and wilted foliage. Which was perfect because, since the explosion, death was all she saw.

Her body jerked as the door creaked, and she turned to see a familiar girl walk toward her.

"Hi, Kalin," the girl said quietly. "Remember me? Juliette?"

Kalin blinked in acknowledgement.

Juliette looked around. Seeing no one said, "How about I go get us some hot chocolate?"

Kalin found herself nodding yes.

Juliette backed away, her arms out. "Stay right there," she said, closing the door quietly.

Kalin's head turned back to the window. She couldn't imagine why the owner's daughter would seek her out. This kindly girl with the cornsilk hair had her own friends visiting, classmates from some boarding school. Kalin had noticed too that the brother, Danni, had been keeping tabs on her. He seemed nice enough, but she wanted to be alone, or back home with the jagged cliffs and savage seas of western Ireland. But home wasn't safe right now.

Kalin heard a soft voice. "Door? Please?" She jumped off the seat to open it, and there stood Juliette, holding two cups of steaming hot chocolate piled high with fluffy whipped cream.

"Let's sit here," Juliette said heading toward two plump armchairs before the fire. Between them stood a small table covered with a linen cloth. Juliette put down the mugs, then pulled a fat cloth napkin from a skirt pocket. The napkin opened to reveal two crusty scones.

Despite her lack of appetite, Kalin felt her tummy growl, and she pressed a hand against it. She sat on the edge of the chair.

Juliette smiled. "Chef Marie's scones do that every time. Wait till you taste the hot chocolate. She makes it and the cream from scratch."

Kalin watched Juliette sip and waited for her to speak. This girl was up to something. Otherwise, why bother with someone who might be gone soon.

"Kalin, where do you go to school in Ireland?"

"I'm homeschooled." Kalin's voice was a scratchy whisper, as if from lack of use.

"Homeschooled. That must be lonely." Juliette's smile seemed sincere.

A long silence filled a clumsy void.

Then out of the blue, Juliette said, "My friends and I have been solving mysteries. We call ourselves the paranormal detective team. Last semester we solved a ghost mystery."

Kalin didn't expect a conversation like this and felt her curiosity growing.

"What ghost mystery?"

Juliette leaned forward. "Our friend Charlotte, who's visiting, was possessed by a ghost. Turned out the ghost was her ancestor, haunting her since she was five years old. It made her life crazy. We helped to release the ghost, and she's better now. Charlotte, that is. The ghost is gone."

Kalin's face, dominated by those deep green eyes, formed a question mark. "How did you know she was haunted?"

Juliette sat back. "You ... you might think this is strange, but I see people's auras."

Kalin's eyebrows jolted upward, but she didn't speak.

"And when I studied Charlotte's, I saw a young woman hovering around her. It was there a lot." Juliette went quiet and took several sips of chocolate.

Kalin felt herself squirm as Juliette's eyes bored into her, up and down, side to side, as if searching for something. Was she herself being examined? Was this girl looking for her aura? Or something else? This was more than a get-to-know-you, friend date. It was a let's-see-how-weird-Kalin-is ploy. She stood abruptly, and thick, brown liquid spilled onto her hand. She tapped her wet palm on the cloth next to the brown ring from the cup. "S... sorry. I'm ... so sorry," she said and bolted from the room.

"Kalin, wait!" Juliette called out, following her. "Please."

Ignoring her, Kalin raced up two flights to her tiny garret at the back of the inn. She slammed the door and fell onto her bed. A cloth doll with hair made from orange yarn lay on the pillow.

She took the doll in her arms and held tight. The figure had been made in the likeness of her brother, Finn.

~

Juliette was stunned to have upset Kalin so badly. Tearfully, she cleared up the mess and brought everything to the kitchen. Then she climbed the stairs to her own room. As she opened the door, Lil, Charlotte, and Aimée rushed toward her, tossing out questions like incoming shafts at a dart board.

The door opened again and Danni slid into the room. "I saw Kalin run upstairs. She looked kind of spooked. What happened?"

"I've ruined everything!" Juliette wailed.

Aimée took her sister's hand and led her to sit on the bed. "It can't be that bad, Juliette. You never have an awful effect on people." Unlike me, she thought.

Juliette's voice shook. "There's a first time for everything."

"Breathe, Juliette. *Oui?*" Charlotte's voice was songlike. "Tell us what happened. Maybe together we can fix it. We've proven we're good fixers."

Aimée nodded and squeezed her sister's hand. Even Lil forced a hopeful half-smile.

Juliette breathed in their sympathy. Before long, she was able to repeat every word of her short conversation with Kalin.

"You've got to get her into that school," Danni said. "Nothing will bring her brother back, but maybe you can help her face his death."

"His murder, you mean," Lil said.

"Right. Let's not forget the mysterious explosion," Aimée added.

"But how will I bring up the Abbey now? She won't ever meet me again."

"Charlotte, how did you get into the Abbey?" Danni asked.

Charlotte pushed stray hairs back into her honey-brown coiffure. "My parents learned about it from some ancient healer who lives nearby. At first, I refused. Why go to a strange place where I didn't know a soul?" She paused, remembering how every time her ghost became active, she'd fall into an embarrassing stupor. "I had to drop out of school. Maman was worried sick and sent me to every doctor in France. No one could figure out what was wrong." She shrugged. "So, they made me go to the Abbey."

Aimée jumped up, her own once perfect side braid now in shambles. "Maybe that's it. We get our parents to talk to Kalin's parents. Papa can be very convincing."

Lil had been pacing and stopped. "Not good. Kalin would feel forced, and then she'd hate us and hate the school."

"I have to agree with Lil," Charlotte said.

Lil grinned. "See? I might not be all warm-hearted like you guys, but I know some things." She held a hand up.

Charlotte slapped it, then said, "I have an idea. Let's wait to see if Kalin comes to dinner tonight. If she does, I could talk to her about my experience. If she doesn't, then we'll sleep on it. There's nothing more we can do tonight."

"I'm not good at waiting," Aimée said, thumbs twirling rapidly.

"We know," Lil said, groaning.

Charlotte checked her pendant watch and stood. "It's dinnertime now. Patience, remember? We had to use that a lot last term. One night of waiting isn't going to kill us."

~

The girls ambled down to the dining room. It was Sunday night, and they'd been invited to join the guests instead of eating in the kitchen with Chef Marie. Danni was invited too, but he didn't like crowds so stayed behind.

Gussied up for dinner, guests walked into the elegant room, chandeliers shimmering. Some folks held drinks, and others looked hopefully at cell phones, although service here was unreliable. Families and friends sorted themselves out at candlelit tables.

Aimée pointed to an empty table in the far corner, and the detective team made their way to it, its position perfect for spying on the room.

Which Lil quickly scoped out and then whispered, "I don't see Kalin anywhere."

"*Non*," Aimée agreed. "See the redheaded woman sitting between my parents? Wearing a jade-green dress? That's Kalin's mother. The man with the beard next to Papa is her father."

Kalin's mother leaned over to Celeste. Kalin's father ignored the conversing women and fired searching glances around the room. His sweep landed at the girls' table; then he looked away dismissively.

"He doesn't look very friendly," Lil said. She knew a snub when she saw one.

Charlotte took a sip of lemon water. "He seems to be in a bad mood. Kalin's mother looks approachable, though."

Juliette, who'd been quiet the last hour, sighed. "You're right, she's not coming."

Aimée started to rise. Her sister grabbed her arm. "Where are you going?"

"We couldn't ask for a better time to talk to Kalin's parents. Everyone's right here."

"No!" Juliette squealed. "We agreed to wait till tomorrow."

The more impulsive twin looked at her friends: Lil, shooting darts of disapproval; Charlotte, clasping her timepiece with worry; her sister, scowling displeasure. She dropped into her chair. "All right! But we'll be sorry we didn't take advantage."

The waitstaff rushed in with clattering plates and clinking bottles. Dinner was served, wine poured, and the conversation about approaching Kalin's parents was over.

As good as the food looked, it was mostly pushed around plates.

Each girl secretly wondered if Aimée had been right.

Chapter 7

Someone Takes Charge

The next morning Kalin awoke in a state of panic. She'd had that dream, the same one since her brother died. Sitting up she looked around, feeling punchy. Then, recognizing her surroundings, she took in a reassuring breath.

It's okay, I'm at the inn.

The dream had been so real. In it, her home had blown up in an explosion. By some miracle she'd survived and found herself stumbling around the roofless space, scorched timbers and singed stones all around her. Harsh-smelling smoke plumes drifted in and around the rubble like bitter reminders. Then the downpour of rain came. Always too late.

Still smelling the scalded wiring, she reached for a tissue. She knew from experience the noxious reminder would be with her all day.

How could she go on like this? Terrifying dreams, no friends, parents who didn't get her, a totally empty life. Every night, she prayed for help. Were Juliette and her friends an answer to those prayers? But how can they help me when I can't even talk about what happened? Whenever I try, I see that explosion—over and over—like a bad news story.

Salty tears dribbled into the corners of her lips.

~

Danni and the girls sat down to breakfast. No one spoke, and as the girls sipped morning tea and picked at their food, Danni gobbled up enough for all of them. Chef Marie watched from her perch at the baker's block, her forehead pinched into a map of worry.

After a while and in between mouthfuls, Danni said, "You girls are unusually quiet this morning. What's up?"

"Kalin didn't come down to dinner," Aimée said. "No one knows what to do next."

"I know she didn't. I had to bring her food."

Juliette dropped her braid. "Did you see her?"

"I knocked, but she didn't answer. So, I left everything at the door and shouted that dinner was there. This morning I went up, and she hadn't touched a thing."

"That's what I'm most worried about," Juliette said. "How much longer can she go without food? She's skin and bones now."

Charlotte stood. "I can't eat if Kalin's not eating. I'm going to plead at her door till she lets me in. I'll tell her about school and how much we want her to come back with us."

Aimée leapt up. "I'm coming with you."

Charlotte smiled. "You know I love your spunk. But it's better if I go alone."

"You're probably right," Aimée said grudgingly, and sat down. "You're gracious. I'm about as gracious as a herd of buffalo.

No one disagreed with her.

As Charlotte climbed the stairs to the garret bedroom, she considered how best to approach Kalin. Maybe she'd use the technique she used with stubborn horses—gentle yet persistent persuasion.

She knocked on the door. "Kalin. It's me, Charlotte Mirabelle. I'm Juliette's friend. I have something important I'd like to talk to you about."

At first there was no response, but then the door tipped open, and a pair of electric-green eyes looked out. "Yes?" she asked hesitantly.

"Kalin, please let me come in. I have a story to tell you about something that almost ruined my life." Kalin paused for a minute, then crawled back to bed with arms crossed.

At least she's not kicking me out, Charlotte thought, as she pushed open the door and stepped into the room. She sat in a chair near the bed and handed over a strawberry jam croissant and a mug of honeyed tea. Giving Kalin a firm nod, she said, "I'll tell you my story after you eat."

Kalin's stomach moaned, and she grabbed the pastry, practically swooning as she bit into the warm croissant.

Charlotte watched her eat. She herself had had few friends growing up on her parents' estate. For one thing, royalty had gone out of fashion in the twentieth century. They were just people, after all. And much worse, no one understood her illness. Of course, even she had no idea she'd been possessed by a ghost. All the same, her affliction made her different from everyone else, a total outlier. Although she and Kalin came from different backgrounds, she felt a bond.

Croissant gone to crumbs, Kalin asked, "What's this story you have to tell me?"

Charlotte took in a bracing breath. "It's not easy to describe, but I'll give you a little history. Since the fifteen hundreds, our property in France has been haunted by the ghost of an ancestor, the very first duchess of Brivalle Castle, Charlotte Mirabelle."

Kalin's face lit up. "You're a duchess? You have the same name."

"I do. My mother is the current duchess descended from her. Over the centuries, people have seen her ghostly figure wandering the grounds. She wears a pale-green gown, and over time became known as the Lady in Green. The story goes that the first duchess was fifteen when her husband murdered her—choked her with his own hands."

"Why?" Kalin knew about murder, her own bleak memory lurking. She swallowed hard and nodded for Charlotte to continue.

"When I was five, I fell asleep in the grass of the castle cemetery. That's when the Lady in Green took possession of me. Afterward and for years, she'd put me into these trances where I couldn't see or hear anything around me. Now I realize she was trying to reach me—to help her escape to the afterlife. But over time, the stupors got so bad I had to leave school."

Charlotte paused, remembering those horrible days. "I was forced to visit the most hideous doctors. Mostly ancient men with beards and enormous bellies."

"Gross," Kalin said.

"Totally gross. Nothing they tried worked. Hypnosis. Antidepressants. Talk therapy." She laughed. "I wouldn't talk, so that was useless. Then my parents learned about the Abbey and forced me to go. At first, I tried to run away. But it actually was the best thing." She smiled conspiratorially, "Lil and the twins helped me free the ghost!"

"So, just like that, the ghost vanished?"

Charlotte walked to the window. "It wasn't easy. It was scary and hard. We had to get help from a wizard." Charlotte laughed. "I know this sounds crazy, but a wizard who actually lives in the middle of a forest."

Kalin frowned. "Are you making this part up?"

Charlotte looked offended. "I would never make any of this up."

"Sorry. Go on."

Kalin joined Charlotte at the round window. "So, how did you get rid of it ... the ghost?"

"I'm not sure exactly—some kind of supernatural magic spell."

Kalin shrugged and climbed back into bed. "No magic can help me. It's too late for that."

"I believe we can help you."

"How?"

"First, by being friends who can relate to someone suffering from an ordeal."

Kalin sniffed. "What ordeals have they ever faced?"

"I don't think Lil would mind my telling you. Both parents abandoned her. She's lived at the Abbey since first grade. And the twins—their father's away a lot and their mother hasn't time for them. They don't talk about it, but I see the hurt. Danni too. Until last summer he was living on scraps, practically raising himself when the twins' family adopted him. And you know about my challenges."

Kalin stared out at the grayness. Could this school help her? Was this the answer to her prayers?

"We want you to come with us," Charlotte said emphatically, "if for no other reason than to be with friends who care." She opened the door. "Come with us, Kalin. You won't regret it. I'll come up later. You must have a hundred questions."

With a kind smile, Charlotte gently closed the door. She had a good feeling about this.

Chapter 8

The Abbey

After Charlotte left, Kalin closed her eyes and emptied her mind. A vision poured in. She was somewhere familiar—on an important mission with these girls. The task was scary and complicated, but in the end, everything turned out right. Although, in her mind's eye, the mission itself was vague, her skin flushed with a surge of hope for the first time since the explosion.

She now had no excuse but to crawl out of this hazy hollow she'd been living in. After all, she was no little worm of an Irish lass born to sit and watch the world go by. She was Kalin MacCumhaill descended from Fionn MacCumhaill, the first king of Ireland, married to Muirne, first daughter of the Druids. Legend said they shared a number of gifts: visionary intuition, great wisdom, heroic courage.

Things were going to get better. She realized a wizard's magic wouldn't bring Finn back. But having friends who understood what she was going through truly was an answer to her prayers.

In this sudden moment of clarity, she jumped off the bed and ran to her parents' room to beg them to let her go to the Abbey. In two minutes, she spoke more words than she had uttered since Finn's accident. "You have to let me go," she insisted, telling them what she knew about the place. Which in truth was very little. She had no idea, for example, that the school existed in another dimension of time. But she didn't care about the details. She was going.

"Ask the twins' parents if you need to know more," she said. "I want to go. These girls like me, and I feel safe with them."

Far from needing to be convinced, her parents were so relieved that even if the school had been run by a tribe of Mongolian sheep herders, they would have agreed.

Thrilled by her parents' quick assent, Kalin ran down the stairs to find the girls. She caught up with them in Chef Marie's kitchen downing a lunch of cheese omelets and café au lait.

"Guess what?" she blurted. "I'm going with you. To the Abbey!"

Joyfully, the four girls jumped from the table and rushed over for a hug. Danni pumped an arm, but remained bent over his plate, scooping food into his mouth lest it get cold.

"So, what's the plan?" Aimée asked. "Do you have to go home first?"

"No, I'll travel with you. My parents will fly home. I don't need much, right?"

"Right," Lil said. "The school provides uniforms. Well, they're not really uniforms, they're outfits that all look the same, but they're kind of cool. Cobalt-blue tunic tops with loose navy pants and purple sweater hoodies. And we have an amazing library, and home cooking." She grinned. "And a stable full of wonderful horses. What else do we need?"

Charlotte flew into duchess-in-training mode, tapping her fingers together. "All right. Here's what we'll do. I'll call my parents. Gustav will drive us. We'll give him a list, and he can stop to pick up anything we're missing. We all leave from here. Together."

Everyone beamed with excitement so brilliant it found its way to Chef Marie who giggled, although she understood not a word. Aimée hugged her sister, too overcome with relief to utter a word.

On the other hand, Danni's stomach felt as if it had been punched by a fistful of loneliness. Yes, his dream of Kalin going to the Abbey had come true. But soon he'd be alone. Again.

∼

On the following Sunday, a black limousine pulled up in front of the inn. The girls filled the car's trunk with their belongings and, one by one, crawled into the back seats. Juliette set down a basket of warm muffins prepared for them by a teary Chef Marie. Not wanting to drag out the good-byes, Charlotte motioned to Gustav, and the car drove away from the waving parents. The twins turned their faces to Danni, who stood next to Celeste on the porch. He managed to lift a hand and blow a somber kiss. Surprising herself, Lil blew one back.

Inside the limo, the girls had chosen their seats. Kalin sat between the twins, Charlotte and Lil facing across.

Juliette communicated with her sister in a private language they called mind-speak. *We need to tell Kalin about the vortex. If we don't, she might freak while we go through it.*

You're right. Who should tell her?

Lil, whose own sixth sense kept her tuned in like a human antenna, said, "Are you two mind-speaking again?"

Kalin snapped her head back and forth. "Mind-speak? What's that?"

"Well now," Charlotte said. "There are some things we need to explain before we get to school. Actually, there's a lot we haven't told you." Seeing Kalin's face go pale, she quickly added, "But it's all good." Charlotte looked at the others. "Wherever do we start?"

Everyone went quiet, wondering how to explain the inexplicable. Their own unusual super gifts. The quirks and peculiarities of the Abbey. The mysterious sisterhood. And most important, that the school existed in the seventeenth century. And that's where they were going, through a swirling, churning, physically unsettling, dimension-shifting, timeline vortex.

"Mother Mary, just tell me," Kalin insisted, Irish lilt intensifying.

"We don't want you going comatose again," Lil said.

Kalin's shoulders dropped. Is that what she'd been like to them? A zombie?

Charlotte put up a hand. "Let me. Please."

The others breathed a sigh of relief. No one could relate to Kalin like Charlotte could.

Chapter 9

Danni Eavesdrops

Shoulders stooped, Danni trudged back inside the inn. Kalin was gone now, and there was no longer anyone for him to watch over. He still believed she was in danger and wasn't sure how, but he vowed to find out. He had to continue helping to solve Kalin's mystery. Remaining in detective mode all day, it wasn't long before he did uncover a clue—that same afternoon in fact—a clue to Finn's death.

Since Danni was considered "the help," guests rarely noticed his presence. He had entered the library to add logs to the dying fire, and there sat Kalin's parents, lounging on the cushioned window bench. Their voices lowered to a whisper when he walked in, but his ears were sharp and his memory keen. Their conversation went like this:

Kalin's dad: "They'll never find our little lass now; she's safe. These Frenchies tell me the school is more hidden than a village in the Amazon."

Kalin's mom: "When we get back, I want to search again for Finn."

"Why don't you admit it, our boy is dead."

She held a hankie to her mouth making a weeping sound. "I ... I won't believe it till they find his body."

"You heard what our daughter said. Well, what she screamed over and over. She saw his skiff explode, for damnation's sake. And we found pieces ..."

"It doesn't make sense," she cried. "Kalin was nowhere near that explosion."

"You know she sees things, dear. Yes, yes, at first, I thought it was bunk. But her visions have proven out every time, haven't they?" His chest puffed out. "Our little Kalin takes after my Celtic ancestors. As did our son." He stared out the window. Then, "I'll never forgive myself for asking him to spy on that degenerate Chester. Nearly fifty casks went missing in the last year. That we know about. I know that scoundrel is in the thick of it."

His wife blew her nose. "Why didn't you just fire him?"

The old man groused, his accent deepening, "I wanted to catch them in the act, is why. If he and others are stealin' from us, they'll be workin' for that damnaigh underground. Those damnaigh Corkys! I'll want to be takin' them all down!"

She stifled another cry. "Your decision may have killed our son."

Their words faded as Danni left the fire and closed the door behind him. He ran directly to his room to write everything down. After their visit to Madame Villars, he'd confirmed that the casks in the waterfall's image did belong to Kalin's family, one of the largest whiskey distillers in Ireland. More than once while at the inn, he'd seen Kalin's father step outside and look around, as if worried someone had followed them here.

Danni had to get this new evidence to the girls. He reviewed his notes before composing a letter telling them what he'd learned. I should be at that school, he thought. It didn't escape him that this time it would be the man who stayed behind, worrying about the women.

Chapter 10

Arrival at School

THROUGH THE VORTEX

Kalin didn't go comatose learning about the peculiarities of the Abbey. In fact, the opposite was true. As every oddity was described—students with paranormal gifts, a secret sisterhood, an old man with glowing eyes, a giant pet falcon—she felt increasingly durable, as if growing a backbone. Well, she already had a backbone, but a stronger one. It was as if, just by the telling, she was absorbing all the strengths, all the gifts, all the gumption of everyone at the Abbey.

But even with all that, she'd not been ready for passage through the timeline vortex, although the girls had done their best to describe what it was like. Being shot like a bullet through four hundred years of time had left her dizzy, disoriented, and shaking from head to toe.

Part of the problem was not knowing the exact moment the blowy cyclone would engulf her. When it did, pow! She'd grabbed the twins' hands and squeezed hard, as if juicing lemons.

"Kalin," Charlotte shouted afterward. "Are you okay? You look dreadful."

"Is it over?" Kalin cried, eyes slammed shut. "I'm still spinning, and fireworks are going off in my brain."

"You can relax now," Lil reassured her. "We've passed through. The first time's the hardest. I've been making that passage since I was five. You'll get used to it."

Kalin let go of the twins' hands. "Make Gustav stop. I'm going to spew."

Charlotte tapped on the separating glass, and Gustav swung the car to the edge of the dirt road. Barely waiting for the car to stop, Kalin jumped out and ran into the woods.

"Not too far in," Charlotte shouted, right behind her. "This forest is practically prehistoric. Think Jurassic Park. With wild boars instead of dinosaurs."

Kalin stopped short and then lost her breakfast. Afterward, she coughed and cleared her throat. "Phew. I'm actually better now. My tummy has always been weird." She wiped her mouth with Charlotte's hanky. "I can't eat when I'm stressed. That's why I'm so skinny."

"But you're better now, right?"

Kalin stood taller, and her face pinked up. "Fit as an Irish fiddle."

Charlotte waved assurances toward three anxious faces glued to the car windows. "The Abbey's cooking will put fat on those bones." Just then, something in the wooded distance caught her eye and she bushwhacked over to it. "Is that what I think it is?" Charlotte said.

Kalin thrashed over bushes and stopped near her, below a dead tree. "What do you see?"

Charlotte pointed up. "See the massive bird up there? That bird is my friend, Hotspur." The bird shrieked an ear-piercing hello and then flew away.

"What ... kind of bird? That wingspan is a wide as I'm tall."

Charlotte's medallion warmed up and she glanced around. "I think the vortex is close by. The old wizard in the woods? She keeps an eye on it through an enormous crystal. Hotspur is her pet bird. She must have called it back." Charlotte looked at the car and the waiting faces. "One second, I have an idea." She pulled a braid of hair from her skirt pocket. It came from the tail of her favorite horse, Bolt. "I keep this for good luck, but I have a feeling it will be a good luck charm of another kind." She tied the braid to a thick branch of the tree and said, Let's go."

Little did she know this single, spontaneous action would become vital to the team.

Kalin shook her head as she trotted behind Charlotte. The strangeness of these parts was beginning to sink in. Knowing she'd get more detail once at school, she didn't ask about the bird, the wizard, or why Charlotte had left the odd strand of hair. Strange, but in a way that she found exhilarating. Still, she had a question that couldn't wait. "The driver, Gustav ... he didn't notice the vortex. Why?"

"For some reason, adults don't register the timeline change. They think we're living in an antiquated, French abbey in the woods. We think it's because adults have lost their belief in the supernatural. Just because something can't be seen, though, doesn't mean it's not there."

Kalin thought about that. "I'll never stop believing," she said. "If I can survive being hurled through time at the speed of light, I can survive anything this place throws at me."

~

A wizened old woman chortled as she peered into a huge crystal, watching Charlotte and Kalin climb inside the shiny, black chariot. Her glaring eyes bulged slightly—black with yellow orbs. Two snowy-white braids framed her face, the dry plaits frizzled as if hit by a jolt of electricity. The old woman clasped her hands together gleefully and gave off a throaty laugh. "In me old bones, I sense a new mystery coming, my dearies. How gratifying … how engaging for this nearly forgotten wizard. You young'uns will soon learn what's to be survived." Then she touched the stone and called home her bird.

~

The abbess, Mother Sophia, watched as the sleek, black limo drove in under a columned overhang at the front of the Abbey. The woman wore a colorful tunic that fell to her knees over loose pants. Her ebony hair was held back by a cobalt scarf matching the tunic. She was tall and imperious looking with feet planted firmly before two enormous wooden doors engraved with winged cherubs and frightening gargoyles.

A peephole in the door opened, then slid shut. Slowly, one heavy door whined open, and stepping through was a weathered old man with shoulder-length white hair and a thick, white moustache that had overgrown to touch his hair. He moved outside slowly, a wooden staff guiding his feet onto the stone deck. The old man's black cape seemed to float outward as it lapped against black-booted feet. Eyes beneath thick white eyebrows emitted glimmers of light.

The trunk of the car popped up, doors flew open, and a gaggle of girls tumbled out squealing hellos and missed yous. The new girl with hair the color of a burnished sunset twisted her head around, taking in the ancient citadel and its two stewards.

"*Bonjour, mes enfants,*" the abbess said. "We missed you, my dears. *Et voila*, Keeper, so much that he's come to greet you. A rare occasion, indeed."

The old man's lips pulled back to reveal a gold tooth that glistened even in the shade. Lil and the twins engulfed him with all six arms. Charlotte hung back, content to smile and observe.

"Is this our new addition?" Mother Sophia asked, as she leaned into the car through the open door. "Come out, my dear. We understand your skepticism." She extended an arm, and Kalin took hold, allowing herself to be pulled from the car.

"Let me see you," the abbess said, looking Kalin up and down. She touched her short, scarlet locks. "I admire your hair. It seems to have its own force field."

Kalin gasped to herself. What a peculiar thing to say. How did people this far back in time know about force fields? "Thank you, Mother." She'd been told how to address her.

"They like to be called *Mother*," Juliette had said. "It helps with loneliness."

By now, Gustav had pulled all the suitcases and bags from the trunk. He bowed slightly, said, "*Au revoir*," and slid into the driver's seat. The girls waved as the sleek black car drove off.

You don't need to know why at this point, but Gustav rejoins the story later, and in a big way. He's not at all what you think he is and you'll learn his story soon enough.

Back at school, and once inside the entrance hall, Kalin was formally introduced to Keeper, in the midst of noisy welcomes and a tumble of gear. He took her small hand in his. "Young lady, you are a dazzling enigma." His voice was gravely like burnt toast.

Kalin had no idea what the word *enigma* meant, but she vowed to look it up as soon as she could get to that amazing library the girls had told her about.

Chapter 11

The Invisible Librarian

THE ABBEY
SEVENTEENTH CENTURY, YEAR 1659

Kalin dragged her bags up four long flights, trying to keep up with long-legged Lil. Her own legs felt like jelly. Probably weak from not eating enough. Why doesn't this monstrous labyrinth of a place have an elevator? she wondered. Then it struck her. It would be centuries before elevators were invented. Hints of lavender came from oil-burning lamps that lined the walls. Later she would learn the sisters burned herbal essences to hide the old-age smell of the monastery. By 1659, the school was already three hundred years old.

Lil led her down a confusing maze of dimly lit corridors to her room. Elevators weren't the only thing Kalin missed. There was no central heating and, being January, it was frigid.

Once in their room, Lil said, "Come, stand by the fire." She held her hands close. "Helpers restock the wood, but we keep it stoked."

Shivering, Kalin wrapped her arms around her torso. "All day and all night?"

"I know. It's a lot to get used to at first. When it's really cold, we run up between meals and classes." Her head tilted with her signature grin. "Now that you're sharing, we'll split fire duty."

Kalin looked around the cozy suite. Over-sized tapestries in vibrant greens and calming sunset colors hung along the walls. The floor was covered by a large rug in a kaleidoscope of comfort. Kalin brightened. "I love your wall hangings. They add charm to these cold walls."

"Thanks. I brought them from home. No one's there to appreciate them."

Someone had brought in a second bed, yet there was still plenty of space in the suite. Drawn by flashes of light, Kalin stepped up into an alcove closed in on three sides by stained-glass windows.

Glass panels flickered the sun's rays around the room in myriad colors.

"Are you sure you don't mind sharing your space?" Kalin asked. "You've been solo so long."

"To be honest, I hated the idea at first. But you seem easy to get along with."

"Easy to get along with," Kalin repeated. "That's what Fi—" She put a hand to her mouth. "I haven't said his name out loud since the explosion."

Lil joined her in the alcove. "Don't push yourself, Kalin. I can barely talk about my mother, and she left many years ago."

Kalin nodded. "Your room is so far away from the others."

"When I first got here at five years old, I did nothing but wail twenty-four seven. It kept everyone awake, including the mothers. So my father hired villagers to restore a room here in an unused wing. I got to make all the noise I wanted." Stroking her white-streaked ponytail, she remembered how good it felt to scream at thunder during storms. "But ... I've been flying solo long enough."

"How old is this place anyway? It seems ancient, even now. And anyway, where are we? Someone said late sixteen-hundreds?"

"I can't keep track, but we're somewhere in the sixteen-fifties. If you can believe it, this hulk went up in the thirteen-hundreds. Over the years, it was used as a nunnery, a hiding place for daughters not wanting to marry some crusty, old man. Or worse, sold into slavery. Since then, whole wings have gone to ruin. Kind of shows how old Europe is in our timeline back home." Lil thought but didn't add that this was more her home now.

Kalin started to ask if the Abbey still existed in the future but a knock sounded.

It was Aimée. "It's us. Open up."

"You wanted to go to the library," Juliette said. "How about right now?"

"Stop that!" Kalin said, grinning.

"Stop what?"

"Reading my mind."

"You said so, out loud."

"No, I didn't. I just thought it." Kalin turned to Lil. "Do you mind if I go?"

"You're on your own, kid. Anyway, I'm headed to the stables to see my horse." Lil slipped on her riding boots and left. "Say hi to Gabby for me."

"Who's Gabby?" Kalin asked. She shivered as she slipped on the purple school sweater and pulled up the hood."

"You'll see," Aimée said with a mysterious smile. "Let's go."

They rushed down one flight to the library. Looking around, Juliette was relieved to see the room was empty. Perfect. Their library sprite didn't usually venture out with people around.

Kalin looked up, "This. Is. Amazing. And so pretty." Burning candles were set all around the room, even in chandeliers. Their warm glow illuminated the vaulted ceiling painted with stars and planets and spiraling galaxies. Wood-planked floors were polished to a high sheen, and exotic rugs were placed around, adding to the cozy quietude. A low-burning fire crackled inside an immense stone hearth, lending the room a mystical atmosphere. It was amazing what you could create without glaring lightbulbs.

The twins led Kalin around dozens of book stacks that soared up to the high ceiling. A rolling ladder stood nearby, offering access to the tallest shelves and to a loft of more stacks.

Aimée pointed to the far end, to a makeshift laboratory with a variety of arcane equipment. "The sisters use all that stuff to make remedies and who knows what else. We use it sometimes too."

A set of copper scales with perfectly level hanging plates sat next to long glass pipes that ran to and from flask-like fixtures suspended over more candles. These weren't lit. The lab looked like a movie set about a mad scientist. Gawking, Kalin started toward the long lab table.

"Not now," Juliette said, and drew her to a different table hidden behind several bookcases. "You'll learn to work that place soon enough." Then she called out, "Gabby, are you here? Aimée and I missed you. We want you to meet a new friend who needs your help."

They heard a chortle of laughter, proof she was nearby. Then suddenly, she popped into Juliette's view, the only one who could see her. Gabby wore a sky-blue dress covered with a white pinafore apron. A tall headpiece lowered a shimmery veil down her wavy blond hair.

"There you are," Juliette said, pointing to an empty chair. "Gabrielle, meet our friend, Kalin, a new student. And she's from Ireland!" Whispery sounds came from the chair.

"What's she saying? Aimée asked, wishing she had her sister's gift of seeing and talking to ghosts.

"She asks if Kalin is running away from the English. She knows people are dying of starvation there."

Kalin's stomach lurched in surprise as she remembered her country's history. Everyone had to learn it in school. In the 1600s, the English pushed their way in, and massive numbers of people did starve. But that was then, and this is now. Wait. Then is now, she realized, feeling a bit disoriented. I'm in France when the Irish are fighting the English back home. *Unbelievable!*

Then she gathered herself and spoke in the direction of the empty chair. "Gabrielle, I come from the future, and that war is over. Now we grow lots of food and have cows and milk and butter. So, people eat better."

"Gabby asks why you're so skinny then," Juliette said.

"I … well … there's another reason for that. I'll tell you some time." She heard a reassuring whisper from the chair. "What I need right now is to find a simple dictionary," Kalin continued. Arms up, she looked around, hopelessly. In seconds, a book moved through the air and dropped into her hands.

Juliette laughed. "Gabby says to look at page two-seventeen. Your word is there."

"This is the best," Kalin said. "A library with an invisible librarian." She set the book down on a nearby table and opened to page 217. As she scanned the page, she remembered from her parents' library of old books that the first printed dictionary had come out in the 1800s. But here, some two hundred years earlier, was a book of words and definitions—hand-written. Had the sisterhood written it?

Sure enough, her word, enigma, was there with this definition: "Something mysterious that seems impossible to understand completely. Example: She is something of an enigma."

Aimée bent over the book. "Why do you want to know?"

"Because that's what Keeper called me when we met, 'a dazzling enigma.'"

"I didn't hear him say that."

"Well, he did. He knows something's out of kilter with me."

"I'm not surprised," Juliette said. "Everyone here has a gift, and Keeper and Mother Weed are master magicians, as you'll learn soon enough."

Kalin shivered, and this time not from the cold. "I see why you say this place is peculiar. But in the best of ways."

"You have no idea," Aimée said with emphasis.

Chapter 12

A Visit to the Wizard

Several weeks went by, and Kalin, still overly thin with strangely cut red hair, settled in to the peculiar ways of the Abbey. Some students, nosy, unfriendly ones, stared and gossiped. Yet, as if sensing something was off, they kept their distance. Was it contagious? And besides, they didn't want to mess with Lil, who was for some reason overly protective of this odd-looking person.

Today, as Kalin stepped out of last class with the twins, Lil met them at the door as she had since Kalin's arrival. Lil, at sixteen, was in a higher class.

Aimée glowered. "We're not entirely helpless. We can protect Kalin, too."

"I know that. But as the Abbey's champion mean girl, you have to admit my presence has discouraged shenanigans." She lowered her voice. "They don't know I'm trying to be a better person."

Aimée blinked in understanding.

"Besides," Lil continued. "I have a message. Mother Weed requests our presence at her cabin. She wants to meet Kalin."

"What? The wizard?" Kalin squealed. "The one who sent away Charlotte's ghost?"

"The same," Lil confirmed.

"How would we get there? She lives in the forbidden forest, right?"

"She does. But the message is from Mother Sophia, so we have permission to go. Keeper's going with us. He'll ride the donkey. He's too old to make it on foot."

"Us?" Aimée asked. "Who gets to go?"

"Our entire detective team has been invited," Lil said. "Which is unusual. I hope she sends Hotspur to guide us. Those woods aren't like ours. It's the land of wild things and killer beasts." She exchanged a look with the twins as they remembered last term. They'd hiked to Mother Weed's cabin alone, disobeying the rules.

Aimée fidgeted. "When do we go?"

"Tomorrow, Saturday, nine o'clock sharp." Lil pulled Kalin toward the back door of the school. "Let's go tell Charlotte before she takes off on Bolt."

"I'm not going anywhere near that crazy horse," Kalin said, working her legs double-time to keep up with Lil's long strides.

Lil spotted Charlotte in riding clothes, walking her horse down the barn ramp. The frisky Appaloosa snorted and bobbed his head, keyed up for the ride. "Charlotte, hold up," Lil said. "We have news. We're getting closer to solving Kalin's mystery."

～

Early next morning, the girls stood by the trail gate at the edge of the forest. On one side of the gate were frosty remnants of the herb gardens. The other side was a thick forest with trees so tall that the girls nearly fell backwards looking up at their peaks.

Kalin's mouth dropped open—she'd never seen such huge trees. Three people couldn't wrap their arms around many of them. Charlotte was right, this was Jurassic Park of ancient Europe. Shines a new light on the word primordial, which she promised herself to look up.

The girls hopped in place to keep warm. "If they don't get here soon," Aimée whined, "I'm starting without them."

"Really, Aimée?" Lil shot back. "You're going in alone?"

Charlotte checked her timepiece. "Give him time. Keeper's old."

A raspy voice sounded from behind. "Who's an old man?" Keeper said, riding up on a donkey, its wide ears perked and tail swishing. "Patience, ladies," Keeper admonished, glaring.

Just then an ear-crushing screech pierced the sky, and a peregrine falcon landed on a branch near Charlotte. Its long, white-flecked wings created an air vacuum as they folded in.

Kalin stumbled back. "Wow! That thing's nearly as big as I am."

"Hello, old friend," Charlotte said. "Remember Hotspur? Mother Weed's pet falcon?"

"I do, but how'd he get so big?" Kalin asked. "Not normal size for a falcon, is it?"

"A story for another time," Keeper said. "If we're late, our gooses will be cooked and eaten for dinner."

That shut everyone up. Charlotte grabbed the donkey's lead line, and the others fell in behind them. Releasing another piercing call, the peregrine flew ahead on the trail leading the way. Kalin's hands flew up to her ears. "Why is he so loud?"

"We like this about Hotspur," Keeper said. "Big and loud. He keeps forest beasts away. You'll be happy to know this bird has made his share of kills. Thanks to him, we'll travel safely."

The bird's knife-like beak and giant claws didn't reassure Kalin, and she stayed as far back as she dared without getting lost. She was a lunch-sized morsel for that bird.

$\sim$

The trip to Mother Weed's took longer at the speed of a donkey, a creature with a pace all its own. Unhurried. Which was just as well for Keeper jostling around on its back.

When the group finally arrived at the cabin, the old woman stood outside, waiting. "It's about time yer here," she groused, throwing up her short arms. "What took youse so long?"

No one answered, as this was her normal greeting, like someone else saying, "Welcome to my home." She opened the door and pointed inside. "You may as well come in," she added, as if she hadn't been the one to issue the invitation. Then she locked her strange eyes onto Kalin's, who had taken a few paces back. "I mean for all of youse to come in," she insisted.

But Kalin wasn't eager to walk past a wizard in a bad mood, and she stood in place, unsure.

The old crone leaned toward her. "You're trying my patience, little one. This is all about you now, ain't it?"

Kalin tried to move, but the old lady was dreadfully frightening, with her frizzled silvery braids, her strings of colored stones and feathers hanging low over cloaks and skirts, and her knobby hands disappearing into pockets as if hiding something. What? A wand? A warty frog?

But then, Kalin felt something familiar pour into her. Ancestral courage. She grew taller and strode by the old woman as if she were no more than a flea. The door slammed shut behind her.

"Now, let's have a look at youse." Mother Weed put swollen knuckled fingers to her chin and circled around Kalin. "Don't be afraid, dearie." Her huge eyes bulged even more than usual. "I'm taking your measure, is all. You might be a tiny scrap, but your energy cloud tells a big story."

"Energy cloud?" Those words again. What exactly did they know about energy in 1659?

"Yes, yes, that," the wizard said. "There's a cloud around us all that stores the shadows of our stories and those of people closest to us.

Keeper and I see yours most clearly. Your chum, here calls it an aura. Ho, ho. What a contraption of a word ... o-rah!" As she laughed at her own joke, her bulbous belly bounced up and down.

A wizard with a sense of humor, thought Kalin, although juvenile.

Aimée, who'd been hovering and probing Mother Weed's every move, piped up, "But how's that different from what Juliette does?"

Mother Weed spun around and leaned into the meddlesome twin. "Well, if it's not our little in-house commentator."

Realizing she'd blabbed again before thinking, Aimée turned away from the wizard's penetrating glare. Aimée had once watched Lil turn into a donkey. Nearly.

But Mother Weed's gaze shifted back to Kalin, ogling her as if examining a specimen in a jar. Kalin could feel herself being pulled into those endless black pupils, ringed in yellow, looking suspiciously like those of her falcon.

Finally, the examination ended, and the wizard looked skyward, as if memorizing what she'd seen. Then she approached Keeper, who sat by the fire. The two leaned in, whispering, staring, pointing, untangling Kalin's mystery in their wizardly way. As they murmured, deduced, and plotted, the atmosphere in the cabin shifted.

The force of their probe made the air buzz and hum, sending waves of eeriness along everyone's necks. Kalin shivered to her bones. What were those two drumming up?

Even the detective team squirmed with discomfort. Thoughts of Kalin's mystery shifted from daring and bluster to apprehension and doubt. While it had been easy to make promises, would Kalin's haunting become impossible to solve?

"Now," the old woman commanded, maneuvering arms and fingers as if gathering air. "Come to Mother Weed. All of you, dearies."

Reluctantly, the girls approached, and Keeper reached for Kalin, drawing her close. "My child," he said in a crusty, wavery, voice, "we have a sturdier sense of things now. For reasons you may not understand as yet, you must go back to Ireland."

"What?" A bolt of dread shot through Kalin's body.

Mother Weed's face flickered a series of unreadable emotions. "Oh, yes, yes, little one. Yer mystery may be solved. But it cannot be solved from here. Oh, ho, ho … no, no. You must go back, dearie. And you must do it soon. The sooner the better." She turned to the group. "Listen well, children. The stakes are high, indeed. But to solve that act of villainy against Kalin's family, you must go to the scene of the crime, and you must go together. The solution lies there and only there. And once there, remember … nothing will be what it seems."

Chapter 13

The Plan

The team hiked home in silence. Even Keeper spoke not a word, so preoccupied was he with the groans of his laboring donkey. The girls' minds filled with questions. Would Mother Sophia let them leave? Where would they stay? How would they even begin to solve Finn's murder?

Mother Weed had said, "Yer mystery may be solved." Wasn't she sure? The magicians had given no further clues or advice, other than to go to Ireland at once. It would be on them to figure out everything else. This new truth weighed on them like a truckload of cement.

Hotspur squawked and screeched away animals as he led them along the path. But the little troupe was far too distracted to notice any threats stalking their heels.

Finally, they passed through the gate and stepped onto school property.

Charlotte spoke first. "Keeper, I'll take you to your cabin. You must be tired."

"Yes, child. I am. Although we need to speak soon with the abbess."

"We will." Charlotte nodded. Although years of duchess training urged her to take over, she worried about being seen as bossy. But someone had to. There was no turning back from the wizards' instructions. "Everyone, go on up to Lil's room. We'll meet when I get back."

Lil and Kalin turned toward school, but Aimée stood at the gate, arms folded. "This feels too weird," she complained. She wasn't usually wimpy, but to go all the way to Ireland? Now?

"Well, we did promise to help Kalin," Lil said.

Aimée hated sounding whiny but couldn't help it. "Let's think about this. Wizards are supposed to be smart, right? But travel to Ireland? Find Finn's killers? Really?"

Lil, who loved the idea of a trip anywhere said, "What's your problem?"

"Well, we just got back. And besides, we're not that kind of detective team."

"Feeling too cozy and comfortable here to help out a friend?"

"That is not—"

Juliette put up a hand. "Stop, you two. We'll sort everything out during the meeting with Charlotte." She grabbed her sister's hand. "Come on."

Lil took Kalin's hand. "We're right behind you."

Kalin cringed at the thought of going back to the scene of her own brother's death. She agreed with Aimée, what could they be thinking? Home wasn't the seventeenth century, with arrows and swords. It was four hundred years in the future, where killers had guns and blew things up.

Finally, the girls gathered in Lil's room and waited for Charlotte.

～

The doorknob gave an old-house creak, and Charlotte stepped in looking like she'd solved the problems of the world. "Ladies, I've got some ideas. But first, let's write down the clues we have so far. Then we'll make a plan."

She's obviously on board, Kalin thought dismally.

Lil lifted the top of her old-fashioned desk and took out a notebook and pen she'd brought from home. She didn't like the coarse paper here, and the ink was messy and smelled bad. "Okay. Where do we start?"

Kalin shuddered. "At the beginning ... the explosion. Mother Weed said things are not what they seem. I'm not sure what she meant, but this damnaigh nightmare started with that."

"Damnaigh," Aimée repeated. "Is that an Irish swear word?"

Kalin's accent thickened. "So, what if 'tis? My da says it all the time. So did Finn."

"If Kalin wants to swear," Lil said, in a way that dared anyone to criticize, "I for one don't blame her. Now, as to clues. One: You saw your brother rowing his boat. In your mind's eye," she corrected. "You don't know where he was exactly, except somewhere along the shore coming to meet you. Two: Right before the vision, you saw that revolting man dock his boat and run off."

"Hey," Aimée said. "That means you can identify him."

A shadow appeared on Kalin's pale face.

Lil continued, "Three: We know the bad man was hiding casks with something stolen. Four: We know your parents brought you all the way from Ireland because you were in danger."

Juliette put a gentle hand on Kalin's. "Right so far?"

Kalin nodded.

Biting her pen, Lil looked out the window, then remembered another clue. "Danni's last letter said your father often went outside while at the inn. He'd look around the grounds, as if someone might have followed you there. At first, I thought your father was mean. But now I realize he was scared."

"I thought Da was mad at me. But when we left for the Abbey, he hugged me so tight I thought he'd break me in half."

Lil poised her pen over the paper. "He was worried. What else do we know?"

"What happened after you saw the ... the incident?" Charlotte asked.

Kalin closed her eyes. "I don't remember it all—it was the end of last summer. I ran home, hysterical. They gave me a sleep tonic, and I woke up later to see Ma sitting by my bed. 'Where's Da,' I asked her. 'Gone to look for Finn,' she said. Da had been practically living at the distillery because the waterwheel kept breaking down. Then I fell asleep again."

"Did they ever find him?" Charlotte asked. "Your brother?"

Kalin's eyes filled up. "Never. He loved to row his longboat up and down the shore. Later I learned the police searched the beaches near our summer house. All they found were pieces of the boat washed ashore."

"The police may be the professionals, but I think we can do better," Charlotte said.

"We can?" Aimée asked.

Charlotte nodded. "We'll go to Ireland on the pretense of working on a special project for school. Like journalists doing research. We're writing a paper on that famous island near you, Skellig Michael. But really, we'll be investigating a murder."

"Good so far," Lil said, already seeing herself exploring hidden caves. "Who notices kids anyway? We'll be able to move around freely."

"I actually agree we can do this," Juliette said.

"You do?" Her sister asked, feeling like they'd switched bodies.

"I do. We have our sixth-sense gifts, right? Charlotte, you'll get Hotspur to come for protection. Aimée, you'll notice if anyone tries to poison us. Lil, your gift of weather control might come in handy, even though it gives you a massive headache. And my premonitions should keep us out of danger. Hopefully."

"See?" Charlotte said, throwing up her arms. "What a grand team we are. Even Mother Weed and Keeper believe in us. We'll be able to find clues the police never did."

"Right!" Lil said. "The bad guys don't know what they're up against." She offered Aimée a challenging smile. "Still want to stay behind? Alone?"

Aimée's eyes widened. "No way. I go where the team goes."

"Good. We're like the musketeers, right?" Charlotte said. "All for one, and one for all. So, do we go to Ireland, or not?"

"Yes!" everyone said.

"What's the plan, then?" Aimée asked, still playing the devil's advocate. "How do we get there? Jump on trains and boats without our parents knowing? Ireland isn't exactly around the corner. And what about the abbess ... she has to agree, you know."

Charlotte pointed. "Lil, keep writing. I've been to Ireland with my parents and know the routes. We take the train from here to Cherbourg on the French coast, about six hours. Then a ship to Dublin. That's longer, overnight. We get a private cabin on the train, and a suite on the ship so we can rest." She stared out the window. "I think my parents would loan us Gustav." She smiled slyly. "Gustav has ... let's just say ... handy experience. If he comes as a chaperone, and we tell them we have Mother Sophia's blessing, all our parents should give permission."

Kalin perked up. "My parents might buy our tickets. Which means opening the summer house on the western shore. We'd have the place to ourselves, except for the housekeeper."

"This might actually work," Aimée said, a little more encouraged.

Lil looked up from note-taking. "Of course, it'll work. We tell our parents the assignment has to be turned in before the end of term. As you know, I don't have parents to worry about, but I'll think of the perfect wording to convince yours."

"Of course, you will. You're our best liar," Aimée said, unable to resist.

"Touché." Lil grinned. "But I call it equivocation." She glanced at the others. "Does anyone know that word?"

"Yeah, we know it," Aimée said. "Being vague on purpose to hide the truth."

"Right. And it'll get the job done," Lil said.

Charlotte stood. "This is good for now. Next, we meet with the abbess. I'll write to Maman, and the twins will write to Madame Celeste. You," she pointed to Kalin, "will write to your parents and request an invitation to visit."

Kalin grinned, her Irish brogue firing up. "We're not as fancy as all that. It's just an old stone house with a bunch of rooms, isn't it?"

Chapter 14

Danni's Streak of Independence and the Talisman

CURRENT TIME
THE INN, AUBERGE DES ÉTOILES

Weeks went by without his pals, and Danni felt more alone than a solo space traveler in one of his drawings. No one here was his age, and though his new mother, Celeste, was kind, he had to have his own adventure or he'd go crazy. Inspired by Lil's white streak of hair, he thought he might look cool with a streak of his own. So on his next afternoon off, he hiked to the village.

Joyeux, like many small villages in France, consisted of a town center and a train station looking the same now as it had 150 years ago. Danni realized that was why people came here and to the inn. To get away from the rush and flash of modern cities.

Now he stood in the central square with its looming church tower and spotted the hair salon. As he opened the door marked Madame Leguin COIFFURE, a bell tinkled. A stylish woman stepped from behind a lace curtain.

"*Bonjour, garçon,*" she said with a high, lilting voice and a friendly smile. "What can I do for you?"

Feeling a sudden pang of shyness, he said, "You used to do Maman's hair."

"Ah, *oui*, you're Danni. I remember your maman." Her smile turned sorrowful. "I'm sorry you lost her, that we all lost her. I remember when you were little." She looked up. "You've grown so much. Come, sit in my chair. I was expecting you, actually."

Danni hesitated. "Expecting me? Why?"

Madame Leguin guided him to her oversized salon chair and brushed his unkempt brown locks this way and that. "You have thick hair; do you want it cut?"

He hesitated, not sure how to describe what he

did want. "*Non*, not cut." Then taking in a quick breath he said, "I want color ... a streak of color."

"*Alors*," she said, showing no surprise. "And what color were you thinking, *mon cher*?"

"Violaceous. It's a kind of purple. Do you know it?"

She laughed. "Of course, I know it. You're being so precise, so creative."

Danni turned toward her. "Can you do it?"

"*Mais oui*. No cut, and violaceous streak coming up. Which side?"

Now he was truly baffled. "I ... I don't know. What do you think?"

Madame wheeled her color tray closer, then swept a black cape over Danni's shoulders. He watched her open two tubes to blend indigo and red. Red? He panicked and tightened his grip on the chair, starting to rise. But Madame's hands had grabbed hold of his head and begun to section off hair with clips. She wrapped some sections in foil, and then dropped a wide paint brush into the bluish-red goop.

Praying she knew what she was doing, Danni closed his eyes and held on tight. The room was quiet except for a dim song coming from behind the curtain and intermittent brushing around foil and hair. What was I thinking? he repeated inside his head. His heart thumped.

After a while, Madame said, "That's enough color, I think. It needs to set." She tapped his shoulder. "I'll be back in a little while. You just relax."

Danni opened his eyes, and she was gone. He snuck a glance in the mirror. Horrific! He looked like a robot head. Down went his eyelids, shutting hard against the bizarre view.

After a good long while, he heard the melodious voice of Madame Leguin. "Well, *mon cher*, let's see what we have, shall we? Come to the sink. And don't leave without my giving you the talisman."

Distracted from his outlandish appearance, he asked, "What talisman?"

"The one from Madame Villars. She asked me to give it to you."

"Huh? You know the sorceress? How did she know I'd be here?"

The hairdresser pulled Danni backwards in the chair and situated his head in the sink. "That woman knows many things," she said tugging away foil and running warm water over his scalp. "Countless things." The warm water helped Danni relax.

"*Bon*," she said finally, dropping the hose. "Back to the chair now. I'll dry it so you don't get cold walking back to the Auberge."

How does she know where I live? Danni wondered as the blowy air tossed his hair this way and that. Does the entire town know everything about me?

"You can open your eyes, Danni," Madame Leguin said. "I think it looks chic."

Danni looked in the mirror and his mouth dropped open. Wavy streaks of royal purple framed each side of his face, much like the color of a twilit sky. He looked way off, definitely not himself. "Will it grow out?" he asked, worriedly.

"Of course, it will. Over time. Don't you like it?"

Danni hopped off the chair. "Not sure," He reached into his pocket for payment. The family was kind enough to give him an allowance.

Madame patted his hand. "My treat. And now, *voila*." She pulled a wrapped item from her apron pocket. "This is from Madame Villars. Don't open it until you get home."

Danni stared at the package then put it in his own pocket. "I won't. *Merci*, madame."

He left the tinkling door behind and ran all the way back to the inn. Happy that the shadows of night would hide his wild idea—for a while, anyway.

Chapter 15

Meeting with the Abbess

BACK AT THE ABBEY
SEVENTEENTH CENTURY, YEAR 1659

It was Sunday, and the detective team had been invited to the solarium for tea. This was a rare event for students, as entry into certain areas of the Abbey was seldom allowed. The solarium was one such place and was marked with a plaque on the door engraved, *"Fermé."* Closed. These inscriptions always emitted a cloak of intrigue and stimulated the curiosity of anyone meant to be kept out.

A few minutes before the appointed time, the girls met in the hallway outside their rooms. Charlotte glanced at her pendant watch. "We have two minutes. I've never been to the solarium before."

"I have," Lil said, with no further explanation. "Follow me." She led them down four flights to Mother Sophia's office and approached a sturdy bookcase at the back of the room. Reaching behind, she turned a wooden lever. The heavy bookcase swung open to reveal a set of stone steps. "This way," she said, urging them through a dim, bone-chilling passageway. Burning lanterns smelled pleasantly of citrus.

As they stepped into a bright expanse, a fresh lushness greeted them, as if it were a summer day. They blinked fast against glaring light that poured into the vaulted conservatory, enclosed by glass panels rimmed with iron frames. On the stone floor, row after row of raised garden beds shimmered a greenness under the sunny blaze. Pungent herbs and sweet spices assailed their noses. Lemons and oranges splashed color against shiny green leaves. An unexpected burst of cheer in midwinter.

"Welcome," came a reassuring voice. The girls turned toward a distant niche to see Mother

Sophia motioning them to her tiny café setup, shaded by tall Ficus trees.

Tea service had been arranged, and Mother Viola, the stocky school botanist with streaky gray hair, stood ready to pour. She wore the same uniform of the sisterhood. But as every sister's tunic and headdress-scarf were unique colors, hers were pine green over the same loose pants. "Come, ladies," she invited with a sense of girlish excitement. "I've made an exotic tea especially for you." She placed a ready hand on the iron pot, as if unable to wait a minute longer to pour.

As the girls approached the cozy corner, lush with flowering vines growing up a trellis, they spotted Keeper relaxing in a padded chair, his gold tooth sparkling as he greeted them. "Stupendous to see you again, ladies. Come. Sit near me."

Each girl selected a wooden chair, set in a half-circle before him. Mother Sophia took a second cushioned seat next to Keeper and nodded to Mother Viola to begin serving tea.

No one spoke until everyone had sipped. Charlotte eyed Mother Viola. "Do I detect a pinch of nutmeg? Such a rarity for this time and place." She thought this sister must be gifted with growing alchemy. Mother Viola blinked a tiny nod as if agreeing with the speculation.

"Girls," Mother Sophia said, "tell me about your visit to the forest. What did you think of the wizard? Have you made a plan?"

Aimée and Lil opened their mouths to speak, but the abbess put up a hand. "First, Kalin." Silenced, the two wiggled back in their seats.

Kalin's face turned red as her hair. Why did she feel small in front of this woman? The abbess seemed kind. And disarming. But kind and disarming in a king-of-the-jungle way.

Keeper covered her hand with his own. "Don't be shy, my Kalin. The abbess may look like a fearless warrior. But her warrior nature is only necessary when the Abbey is threatened."

"Has that ever happened before?" Aimée piped in.

"It has," Keeper said. "These are primitive times. But thanks to the powers of this sisterhood, we've experienced a long age of peace. Now, tell us. What stratagem have you ladies designated?"

"How do you know we have a stra ... er ... plan?" Aimée butted in.

"Of course, we know," the abbess said emphatically. "Your intentions surround every one of you in a penumbra of shadows. But details need words. So, speak up, young Kalin. Are you not descended from the MacCumhaill tribe of Éire?"

Kalin straightened up. "Éire is the old name for Ireland." Then she leaned forward, able to describe their plan, how they'd get to Ireland. "And," she added, "you asked what I thought of your sorceress, Mother Weed." She paused wondering how honest to be. "I have a question, first. Has she ... this wizard ... gone 'round the bend? Is she a little batty in the belfry, as we say back home?"

The adults chuckled, trying to visualize the old wizard through the eyes of young women from the future. They were aware, sadly, that the centuries had suppressed much of the world's magic and the unconventionality of these olden times.

Keeper cleared his throat. "We like to call her eccentric. Now to your plan. Overall, I believe it to be a good stratagem. But along your journey and once there, you must take especial care to protect yourselves from the rascals of your world. In many ways they seem more damaging than villains of our time. We shall worry every wink of time you're gone." He turned to the abbess. "What say you, Sister?"

"I agree with all you have said." Then, she reached into a hidden pocket and pulled out a package wrapped in colorful tissue paper. "And now, here is something for your journey. It's come to us from Madame Villars." Her bright blue eyes beamed. "Your chum Danni sent it."

Charlotte took the package. "What is it?"

"A talisman—a good luck charm, in your language," Keeper said. "A sign you may yet find that treasure at the end of the rainbow. Stories of treasures and rainbows are from Éire, are they not?"

Charlotte carefully unfolded the paper and turned over a flat, brass circle the size of a small compass. "What are these codes and symbols? And look here, it says Michael." The girls leaned in close.

"It's a sigil of Archangel Michael," the abbess said. "This piece is several hundred years old even now, and precious. When cared for with reverence, it will guide and protect you."

"Sigil?" Lil asked. "I've never heard that word before."

Keeper sighed. "I see some of the old words have been lost in time. A sigil is a signet, or seal, usually made of metal, imprinted with symbols some believe to have supernatural powers."

Charlotte threaded the ornate medallion onto the chain next to her timepiece. It warmed slightly against her chest and she beamed internally.

After a second pouring of tea and general conversation about the upcoming trip to Ireland, the abbess gave a sign of dismissal, and the girls left.

Thinking about all that had been said, they climbed the stairs in silence. High stakes? Sigils?

Treasure at the end of a rainbow? People here talked in such riddles. They'd sort them out later. Although they'd received no specific, concrete directions, they had permission to leave school. And they had a mysterious token from Madame Villars. Help was coming from many directions.

Still, it would be up to them to actually solve the mystery of Kalin's haunting.

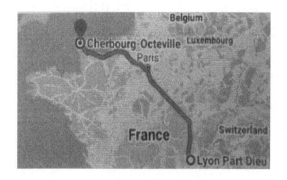

Chapter 16

Onward to Ireland

CURRENT CENTURY, STILL JANUARY
TRAIN STATION, LYON, FRANCE

"We're here," Charlotte called out from the back of the limousine as it pulled into Gare Part Dieu and the train that would take them to Cherbourg. "Six hours in a train is a long ride, but we'll be cozy in the private compartment. Thanks to my parents."

The limo slowed, and Gustav drove into the passenger delivery lane. He glanced at his driving partner. "Help the ladies with their bags, Jorge.

I'll grab my things and give you the keys for the drive back to the manor house."

"*Oui, monsieur,*" the young man said. The junior footman didn't salute, but he wanted to. After all, Gustav had served in French intelligence. Although retired, he still deserved the utmost respect, as did all spies of the realm. Of course, this had never been confirmed by Gustav himself, but everyone who worked at the manor knew, or at least speculated, about his military history. Although unusual that a former spy had taken a job as a chauffeur, Gustav had been with Charlotte's father, the duke, in the Middle East, and had saved his life during a perilous mission. Gustav was now enjoying a peaceful life, where not every incident was a potential death trap. Being a chauffeur was the easiest job Gustav had ever had. Perhaps it was time for a little action.

The vast lobby of the train station opened into a hubbub of noise and conversation as people hustled back and forth, dragging suitcases toward their proper rail platform so as not to miss their trains. Startled animals whined and barked in protest at being pulled along, many against their will.

"Track seven!" Charlotte shouted over the commotion. "Everyone, get out your tickets."

The girls rummaged around their packs to be ready when the conductor made his rounds. Gustav bent over his well-worn duffle bag, unzipped a side pocket, and removed his ticket, sliding it inside the chest pocket of a tweed blazer. Then he picked up a rectangular case and threw the strap over his shoulder, knocking his Irish cap into a jaunty tilt.

Lil watched him suspiciously. "What's in that case?" she whispered. "It looks heavy."

Aimée whispered back, "He's our bodyguard, right? Maybe it's a weapon."

Charlotte shook her head. "*Non.* Probably a special computer like the military uses." Further speculation was interrupted when Charlotte pointed. "There ... track seven. We leave in fifteen minutes. Kalin, how are you? You look a little pale."

"I'm all right. Just nervous about going back."

Gustav reached down from his six-foot height and ruffled her coppery, cropped hair. "You'll be fine, *ma petite*. We won't let anyone hurt you."

"Hmmm," she mumbled. One minute her body thrummed with the fierce courage of her ancestors, and the next she felt like a lost lamb. Right now, mostly the lamb.

The girls and their escort pushed against the flow of arriving passengers, sidestepping people and luggage on their way to track seven. The Cherbourg train sat ready on the rails, chugging in anticipation, its first-class doors open. Everyone climbed aboard pulling bags up the high metal steps.

"This way," Charlotte said, as she led the girls to Compartment 71 toward the back end of the car. The small chamber had facing bench seats, each with a sleeper cubby above. The smell of polished leather permeated the space, and wooden walls gleamed in the sunlight. Tall windows were open letting in wintery air. Charlotte shivered and reached up to shut them.

"Look," Aimée said, pointing up. "We can take naps."

"Leave it to you to think about sleep during what promises to be our best caper yet," Lil said.

Aimée rolled her eyes but didn't respond. She was trying not to bicker with Lil, who, she hated to admit, was often right.

Gustav stood in the hallway observing the girls, his charges for the duration. The smoking car was right next door, and that's where he'd settle in after inspecting all adjoining cars for anyone suspicious. Kalin's father had been explicit about possible danger to the girls. Gustav slipped on a pair of reading glasses that gave him the demeanor of a professor headed for university. A harmless fish, but with a keen eye for sharks.

"Are you joining us, Gustav?" Kalin asked.

"*Non*, but I'll be right next door." He opened a storage cabinet and stashed in his duffle bag and the large black case. Then he locked it and pocketed the key. He held up his phone. "If anyone wants to leave the compartment for any reason, call or message me first."

"We will," Charlotte said. "We'll be fine; we have food and tea. If we need anything else, we'll let you know."

"*Tres bien*," Gustav said. He pushed up his fake glasses, stroked the silver beard he'd grown for the occasion, and strolled off in the direction of the smoking car.

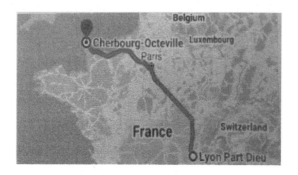

Chapter 17

Shamrock

Gustav slipped into an empty booth of the smoking car, lit a cigarette, and observed people as they passed through on their way to general seating. No one stopped in his car, so he remained alone. After a few minutes, a long, piercing whistle blew, and the train pulled forward.

He finished his smoke, a nasty habit he wanted to quit, and decided now was a good time to inspect the passengers. Everyone was seated, and as he walked up and down the aisles, no one in particular stood out. But once he reversed direction, his eyes fell upon two men he recognized from the train station. He had caught them watching the girls.

One was a young man who held a small, wiggly dog. Next to him sat a gaunt, wiry man with a mat of black hair that could use a shampoo and a face that could use a shave. Both men wore rough clothing and looked like they might do anything for money.

And here they were on the girls' train.

Gustav strolled back toward the first-class car at the end of the line. His thoughts drifted to his satisfaction with the girls' train car being the last one, with only one way in. And anyone would have to walk by him in the adjoining smoking car to get to them. The only downside was the first-class restroom. People would use it when bathrooms in other cars were full.

Along his walk back, as he got closer to the suspicious men, they shifted their eyes away pretending to tend to their feisty dog. Gustav walked by and the little mutt leapt out. "*Oof, petit chien,*" he guffawed, catching the animal. The puffy thing growled, showing pointed teeth.

"Hey," said the young man. "He don't mean no harm, does he? Give 'em back here."

"*Pardonnez moi, monsieur,*" Gustav said with exaggerated manners. "Yes, yes, here take him, please. I am not interested in playing catch with your dog." Gustav dropped the critter into the lap of the young man and walked away mulling over his accent. Most definitely Irish.

No one else seemed out of the ordinary, and Gustav swayed with the motion of the moving train, to Compartment 71. He looked in through the glass window to see all girls present. Some were reading, and others stared out at the passing French countryside. The twin called Aimée was eating a pastry, crumbs gathering on her lap. He grinned. She would be the one to keep an eye on with that reckless personality.

Once back in the smoking car, he ordered coffee and a soggy breakfast pastry from an attendant who had suddenly appeared. No one had packed a delectable snack for him.

∼

Aimée stood up and stretched. "I have to go. And I'm getting claustrophobic." She'd been sitting forever between her sister and Kalin who stared out the window.

"Make sure you come right back," Lil said, giving her the eye.

Juliette reached out. "Wait. Gustav said to message him if we left."

"You worry too much," Aimée said, opening the door. "I'm just going to pee."

They all leaned toward the window and watched her disappear down the hall. Then they went back to what they'd been doing.

Aimée looked up at the red light over the toilet. Occupied. "Ou, ou," she said, crossing her legs. She had to find another bathroom. Fast. Turning around, she crept on by her own compartment and tiptoed through the smoking car, and the next one, and the next, until she finally found an open bathroom. Gustav, with his back to her as he poured sugar into his coffee, had no idea she had just slipped by him.

On her way back, a yipping sound caught Aimée's attention, and she bent to see an adorable dog. "Oh, how cute," she said. The furry white, pug-nosed creature twisted around on the lap of a young man with a mess of red hair. "What's his name?" she asked.

"Shamrock." The boy fluffed the dog's ears affectionately as it whined with pleasure.

"Shamrock! Is he Irish? We're headed to Ireland." As she spoke, the dog jumped into her arms, sniffed her neck, and licked her face. She giggled.

"Who's we?" The young man asked.

"Me, my sister, and some friends. "We're taking the ship tonight, from Cherbourg."

"That's brilliant. We'll be on our way by ship, too. A coincidence, I'm sure, miss."

The train slowed as it prepared for a scheduled stop. "This stop is good timing," the young man said. "Shamrock will be needin' a walk ... to ... you know."

"I imagine he does. We've been riding quite a while." Aimée handed back the dog. But it didn't want to leave her arms. "Poor thing," she said, hating to part with such an affectionate creature that had obviously fallen in love with her.

"I'll tell ya what, why not step outside with us? It'll take a small minute now, won't it?"

Aimée looked around. "I have to tell someone, first."

"Naw, ya don't, dearie. By the time you do, this train'll be movin' again. Lookie there, the door's open. We'll step out, nice and easy, and be back in a jiff like. Right?"

The dog was glued to her now, its fleecy front legs holding her neck. "If it's just for a minute, then." As she moved toward the opening, Aimée glanced back to be sure Gustav wasn't nearby. Maybe he'd never know.

The boy and his older comrade stepped outside. Aimée followed holding Shamrock.

Out of the train.

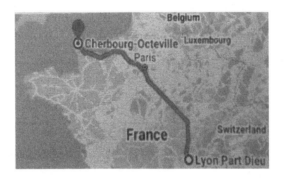

Chapter 18

The Disappearance

Gustav decided to check in on the girls while the train was stopped. As he approached their compartment, loud voices peeled from the small room.

"Go look for her," one of the twins was saying, as she fiddled nervously with her braid.

"She's your sister." He thought this was Lil speaking. The tall, thin teenager with coal black hair, and a prominent nose. She looked quite like a female Sherlock Holmes.

Then his duchess spoke, "Gustav! Aimée is missing. I was about to text you."

The hair on Gustav's neck jumped to attention. "Aimée? What do you mean, missing?" He stared at the other girls. The redhead was pale as a ghost, and the other twin wept quietly.

"She went to the toilette a while ago," Charlotte said, "and hasn't come back."

Gustav ran down the aisle to the first-class restroom at the end of the car. Empty. He stuck his head out the back door of the train car and the wind lifted his hat. He grabbed it. Seeing nothing, he power-walked back to the compartment. "Don't go anywhere," he ordered grimly. The girls nodded; each face tight with apprehension.

Except for Lil, who said, "Maybe someone kidnapped her? Can I go with you to look?"

"*Non.* Stay in this compartment. Close the door and don't let anyone in." He handed Charlotte a container that appeared from an inside pocket. "If someone tries to push in, spray them with this." He rushed down one train car after another to where the suspicious men sat.

Both men and their dog were gone! Following a hunch, he jumped off the train and glanced around the platform. No one. Then he quickly wandered the station grounds looking for where one might take a dog to do his business. A tiny grass park appeared off to the side, and he raced to it, his heart beating like snare drums in a parade. He could not lose one of these girls, especially in the first few hours of their journey.

Aimée looked up from her spot on the grass to see the athletic, silver-haired man running toward her. Her face drained of color and she dropped the dog. "Gustav!" she yelled. "I was just ..."

Gustav pulled a fake pistol from inside his jacket and pointed it at the two men. Throwing their arms up, they backed away. The gun didn't even shoot, but these imbeciles had no way of knowing that.

"Hello, gentlemen," he said with cunning. "We won't have trouble now, will we?"

They nodded in unison, the younger one's head practically shaking off his shoulders. This shenanigan wasn't enough to lose his life over.

"Excellent," Gustav said taking Aimée by the arm. "Come along, mademoiselle. Your break is over." Then he force-marched her back to the platform as he slid away the fake weapon.

"Hey," she cried, trying to free her arm. "I only stepped off for a minute."

"Don't you realize, silly girl, these men were hired to kidnap you?"

Aimée stopped and craned her neck up at him. "You're being totally paranoid."

"My dear," Gustav said, taking in breaths to calm himself, "I've been told by Kalin's father that their daughter is in peril from an Irish crime syndicate. And the same is true now for each of you. I promised to let nothing happen to a single hair on your little heads. I take my job seriously, so if you don't follow my rules, I'll handcuff you to your seat."

Aimée turned red as a ripe tomato. "You'll do no such thing. I'll call Papa."

The train whistle blew, and Gustav led Aimée back on board. "Good idea, *ma petite*. We shall call your papa together, and I'll explain that you left the train with two strange men, and without permission. I've already spoken to all your parents, so I have no doubt they will be most disappointed in your behavior."

Aimée opened her mouth, then shut it. "Hmph," she uttered, but spoke not another word.

In truth, Gustav had no handcuffs with him, but the bluff seemed to work. For reasons beyond his full comprehension, his threats were always taken seriously.

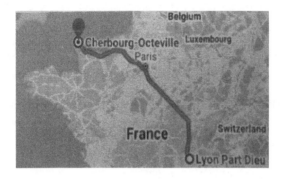

Chapter 19

The Newcomer

Reluctantly, Aimée stepped into the compartment and was greeted by scolding voices and angry faces. Lil yelled the loudest. Juliette sat mum, tears running down in fast rivulets. Kalin's face held a look of terror, and Charlotte, her hands on her hips, uttered words of rebuke as if Aimée were a bad filly who'd thrown her into a mud hole, dirtying her best riding outfit.

"I'm sorry!" Aimée said, with emphasis on the word sorry. As if to say none of this were her fault.

"Whatever," Lil said, "but we'll never trust you again." The others nodded in agreement.

Gustav pulled a private grin as he watched Aimée being reprimanded by her peers. This one wouldn't go astray again for a while. Believing the girls were safe for now, he decided to check the kidnappers' car. Had they reembarked? Or had they ditched the train to Cherbourg entirely?

"Stay here, everyone. I'll be back." Giving the girls a stern look, he left.

As he pushed open the car door where the men had been seated, he stepped into chaos. Fully grown men ran up and down the aisle, shouting and trying to catch a little dog that seemed to be in a panic. These were not the same men. But it was the same dog.

"What's going on here?" he asked in a commanding voice.

A woman at the back of the car leaned out. "*Le chien*, he's causing a ruckus."

"Where are his owners?" Gustav asked, as he made his way to the abandoned seats.

Another passenger said, "No one knows. Someone threw the poor thing on the train right before the door shut. Those two men never got back on."

Gustav sat down in the empty seat and held out his hand. The little mutt stopped barking and ran to him, jumped into his lap, and showered him with doggie kisses.

"Are you the owner?" someone asked.

"*Non*. But I know who was. I believe this dog has been abandoned." He smiled. "And I think I can find it a happy home."

"Take him away, please. I have a migraine," said the same woman at the back of the car.

Gustav tapped his cap and bowed slightly. "*Mais oui, madame*. I am at your service." He stood, and the creature nestled in his arms like a newborn baby.

Charlotte looked up and opened the door when she saw Gustav. "You're back so soon. What's that under your jacket?"

He held out his discovery. "Aimée, I found something you forgot,"

"Shamrock!" She shrieked as the dog flew into her arms, greeting her like its lost mother.

The room turned into a swirl of laughter and cries of delight. Instead of being frightened by the noisy female commotion, the dog gleefully leapt from one set of arms to another, ecstatic to have found not one, but five new mothers.

Well, more like four new mothers. Lil sat stiff and unimpressed by the newcomer. "And what do we do with that?" She glared at the dog, her dark eyes penetrating.

Aimée nuzzled the critter, now back in her arms. "Can we keep it, Gustav?"

"For now." He handed her a bag of dog bits he'd found under the seat. "His owners … your friends," he added with sarcastic emphasis, "have disappeared and left the creature behind."

"We'll take it as far as Dublin," Lil said, "and then look for a shelter."

"*Non!*" Aimée exclaimed, then looked at the others appealingly. "We should vote."

"What do you think, Kalin?" Charlotte asked. "It's your house we're going to."

"Let's see if he gets along with my Siamese cats. If so, then it would be grand."

Aimée held the dog to her chest, feeling its blissful whimpering. She prayed Kalin's cats would approve of their new brother.

Chapter 20

A Note Discovered

The remainder of the trip to Cherbourg was mostly uneventful. The girls ate, read, and slept. No one dared venture anywhere except to the first-class restroom, or to the smoking car where Gustav sat guard like a Roman centurion.

Even the newcomer was quiet, napping mostly, having worn himself out being chased. At all three stops, Aimée took the creature outside for potty breaks, chaperoned by Gustav, who kept a sharp eye out for troublemakers. Lil went too, pepper spray handy.

I did say, mostly uneventful.

Soon after the attempted kidnapping, Gustav enlisted Lil in a search. "I suggest we comb the area around the abandoned seats. Maybe those blackguards left something behind that would help us learn who was behind the kidnapping."

"Good idea," Lil said eagerly, and followed him through multiple cars to where the men had sat.

"And don't be obvious about it," he commanded.

Lil knew exactly what he meant, and began her mission by sitting still in one of the seats left by the rogue men. After a few minutes she dropped something on the floor and bent over to collect it, crawling around to completely search the area.

Gustav pretended to wait for the bathroom so he could watch everyone in the car. He noticed that the woman who'd complained of a headache was watching Lil intensively.

Lil popped into the seat, face red from bending over, and opened a slip of paper. Ignoring Gustav, she pocketed the paper, waited a few more minutes, then stood to make her way back to Compartment 71. As she walked past the woman, she heard a deep, raspy voice.

Lil bent closer, "What's that, *madame*?"

"I said, give me that paper. Please like," the woman added, a touch of brogue slipping in.

"What paper?"

"Don't be evasive with me, young lady. The paper you found and put in that pocket." She pointed to Lil's left-hand jacket pocket.

"You mean this, *madame*?" Lil said in perfect innocence, pulling out her ship's ticket.

The woman was flustered now. "I saw you pick it up. A written note. It's not yours."

"You're wrong, *madame*. I dropped my ticket. Luckily, I found it. See?"

Rising, the woman reached out for Lil's pocket, but Gustav had moved directly behind her. "*Cherie*, is everything all right?" he asked, steel flints behind gray eyes.

"*Oui, Papa*. This woman was confused, is all. *Au revoir, madame*," Lil said graciously, and then walked away.

Gustav gave the woman a threatening look and followed Lil, jostling through connecting car doors where wind whipped around their sudden opening.

When the two arrived at the smoking car, they spread open the hand-scrawled note and read it together.

Unfortunately, some words were smudged, as if the paper had been dropped in the rain and then shoved back into a pocket.

The note said:

Mates,
Take red-headed (smudged word), the boy's (smudge). If no, take (smudge) girl.
Bring 'er down inside the (smudge) near the Muckross (smudge). Leave (smudge) at Crowley's and we'll meet near the stone circle at mi ... (smudge).
If no luck, don't (smudge) for yer payment. We be done with ye.
The boy is sure enough (several words smudged).
Runie

Puzzled, Gustav and Lil stared at each other, then back at the paper.

"Let's bring it to Kalin," Lil said. "Maybe she can fill in some missing words."

～

"Mother Mary save us!" Kalin said, taking in a sharp breath. "I think they were going to take me, or someone, to the underground tunnels at Muckross. Nothing but rotting bones down there. The tunnels used to hide prisoners, but no one goes there now. No one with honest intentions."

She sat next to Lil, who grabbed the paper and pulled it close, studying every word. "Actually, there are lots of clues here," she said, her pupils squeezing tight like camera lenses. "Clues of geography. Where is this Muckross place?"

"It's the ruins of an old abbey near the village, just off the Ring of Kerry. The village is Kenmare. Not far from our summer house."

"Hey," Aimée jumped in. "I wonder if that abbey has a vortex, too?"

"Not important right now," Lil said cryptically. "Kalin, can you fill in these smudges?"

"Maybe … it could mean hide me in the tunnels, near the ruins." She pointed to the last line. "What do they mean about my brother? That he's …?"

Charlotte put an arm around her and drilled Lil with a look. "Let's not go there."

"Right," Lil said. "Not important for clues, anyway. Can you read the rest of the note? Fill in the blanks?"

"I'll try." Kalin took the page and read out loud, her voice shaky.

"Mates,

"Take the red headed girl, the boy's sister. If no, take … take … any? … girl.

"Bring 'er down inside the tunnels near the ... ruins? ... behind the Muckross Abbey. Leave...." she paused, "leave, something ... leave a note, leave word? ... at Crowley's and we'll meet near the stone circle at midnight.

"If no luck, don't ... come? ... don't show? ... for yer payment. We be done with ye."

The words blurred, and Kalin stopped reading.

"That helps," Lil said. "How far are these places from your house?"

"Not far. All in walking distance. Our house overlooks Derrynane Bay and the sea."

"Where's the distillery?"

"In Killarney. About a half hour drive. My da drives back and forth all the time."

Lil squinted in concentration. "It makes sense that if these guys are stealing whiskey, they're hiding it somewhere along the coast. Like we saw in the vision. What about caves there?"

"Yes, caves at the bottom of the cliffs."

Lil looked at Gustav and smiled like a cat who'd caught the mouse.

Gustav nodded with appreciation. "You've got good clues that those imbeciles were careless enough to leave behind. A good start, even before we get there."

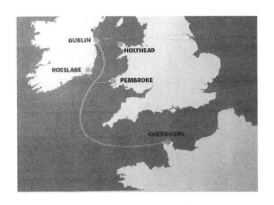

Chapter 21

Ouija Board

The ferry's whistle blew, and the girls watched passengers wave vigorously to people on the French shore. Everyone except Lil covered their ears. With a gleeful grin, she let hers take in the penetrating sound. They were on their way to Dublin!

Having no one to say good-bye to, they hurried to their suite. Gustav followed them and, once inside, surveyed their room. Glaring at Aimée he said, "Do not leave. As I understand it, dinner will be brought to you. You have everything you need."

"But, what about him?" Aimée held up the squirrely Shamrock. "He needs food too, and some place to … you know."

Gustav grunted. "I know that, and I'll work on it next." He left wearing a scowl.

Juliette stared at her sister. *Why do you always fight Gustav's orders?*

The answer seems obvious to me.

Charlotte put up a hand. "You're squabbling in mind-speak again. I can tell. This is a long cruise, so let's all try to get along. We'll give Shamrock some of our food and call on a crew member to take him to do his duty."

"Oh," Aimée said, as the simple solution sunk in.

Juliette said, "Hmmm, I wonder though, where do dogs go on ships?"

The animal in question jumped down and ran to the toilet, where he drank water from the bowl. "Eww," the girls uttered. Except Lil, who rolled her eyes and grabbed the little mutt by the ears, pulling him away. "He'll get water later. For now, I'm putting him on this pillow, on this shelf. And he'd better not move." She glowered at the moppy ball of fur that let out a yip.

Shamrock settled down to watch the girls select their beds and unpack. The twins would share one bed, Lil and Charlotte the other, and Kalin would sleep on the small pulldown.

"Look," Lil said lowering a table from the wall, "We can play cards. It'll pass the time till dinner." She yanked open a drawer and pointed to a stack of games including an old Ouija board. "Haven't seen one of these in centuries."

Kalin stared at the board. "I've heard about these, but our church forbids them. I've never really seen one."

"Not everyone believes it's a game," Lil said. "Some think the board really talks."

"I doubt it," Aimée said. "The makers made that up to sell a lot of them."

Charlotte stayed silent. Never having had friends, she didn't play games.

"I want to try it," Lil said. "It might give us more clues."

"Hmph," Aimée said. "Our own gifts are far better than that charlatan thing."

Lil flipped back her white-streaked ponytail and set up the board. "Charlatan? Is that your word of the week, Aimée? The word charlatan refers to a person, not a game."

"Whatever. I'll just watch."

Kalin sat opposite the Ouija board. "What do I do?" she asked.

"Put your fingertips here with mine. On this wooden thing. It's called a planchette."

"How do you know so much about it?" Aimée butted in.

"My nanny made me play all the time. She swore it told her when Father would show up. She didn't want to get caught being mean to me."

"Did it work?"

"Unfortunately. Now, think of questions to ask."

Charlotte piped in. "How about this? Where should we look for clues in Kenmare?"

"Good one," Lil said, and closed her eyes. Kalin did the same. The planchette didn't move an inch.

"What did I tell ya?" Aimée said, smirking sarcasm.

"Shh," Lil hissed.

The room went quiet, the wind howled around the ship, and after a while the wooden arrow tittered in place. Then it crawled in one direction, then another, and then moved around the board. Soon it began to stop on individual letters.

Charlotte pulled out paper and pen and wrote them down, over time gathering several words. After a half hour of deep concentration and feeling the piece move and stop, Lil lifted her fingers. "We're done. I hope someone kept track."

Charlotte lifted a piece of paper. "Here. Some look foreign though, like … tiaoide and aduantas …? Am I saying those right? Maybe I did it wrong."

Kalin looked surprised. "Those words are Gaelic. Tiaoide means tide, like tidal water, and aduantas means anxious."

"How odd," Charlotte said. "But these others are common words, like food, and fish, and Corkys. But really, none of it makes sense."

Juliette had watched Kalin carefully. "Kalin, is more memory coming back? I bet you saw or heard things you've blocked."

"Maybe," Kalin said. Then her eyes widened, greener than usual. "I was waiting for Finn at the dock. For some reason, he'd been rowing up and down the shore, day after day. He'd not been himself all summer." She shook her head at the list of clue words. "I have no idea what these might mean. And Corky ... that's what we call people from Cork County, right next to our own county."

Lil sighed. "We need way more clues."

Little did they know that clues were about to rain down from the most unexpected places.

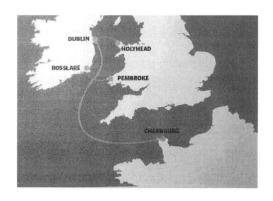

Chapter 22

The Search

Time passed slowly on the ship as Juliette and Charlotte played poker, taught to Charlotte by Gustav when she was five. Aimée was lulled sleepy watching waves peak and froth in the channel. Lil paced and chewed her nails. And Kalin tried to nap but couldn't, mostly worried about what new dreads would greet them once they arrived home.

Gustav checked in on the hour. Precisely.

Finally it was dinnertime, and the girls heard the clattering of dishes outside their door, followed by a knock. "Open up, we have your meals," a man's voice called out.

"We?" Lil asked. Looking through the peephole, she saw two people in serving attire holding trays and opened the door.

A hefty, tall woman and an older, unsmiling man stepped in. They lowered several trays just as Charlotte hurriedly scooped up the games.

The lively woman rubbed her hands together. "Where is this *petit chien* I was told to take for a walk?"

Aimée ran to the bathtub, where Shamrock had taken to sleeping on a pillow. Picking him up, nuzzling, she asked. "Can I come with you? I have to get out of here."

"No!" the others shouted together.

The young woman looked surprised and glanced around. "No? Are you prisoners then?"

"Yes, miss. We are," Aimée said unhappily.

"For our own good," Charlotte added as she led the woman to the door. "Bring him back soon, please." She practically pushed the woman and dog into the hallway and shut the door.

"That was rude," Aimée said. "And you're usually so polite, so genteel."

"I don't trust anyone now, including you," Charlotte turned to the food. "Let's eat."

Lil nodded her approval. Aimée was definitely not to be trusted.

"But I want to know where animals poop on a ferry." Smelling dinner, she sat down to eat. "And save some of those chicken nuggets for Shamrock."

Everyone ate enthusiastically, each girl left to her own thoughts. Charlotte's went like this: how would they continue to manage Aimée's recklessness? Although she kept promising to be less foolhardy, it was obvious the girl couldn't help herself.

A while later, a knock sounded and Charlotte opened the door. There stood the same young woman holding a squirmy Shamrock, not wanting to go back in. "Oops," she said as the dog leapt from her arms and ran down the hall, disappearing around the corner.

As you might guess, Aimée took off after him, also disappearing around the corner. So much for promises made.

Lil threw up her arms. "Great! I'll go after her. Stay here and lock the door." She and the young woman took off after the two runaways.

"I think I know where he's going," the woman said breathlessly, heading toward a staircase. "He met another dog on his walk." She and Lil got to the doggie rendezvous deck and looked around. No dogs. No Aimée.

"Earlier, they ran into the dining room," the woman said, "Begging for food. Let's go there." Dinner was over, but a few people lingered at their tables. "If we wait here, Shamrock may be back." She pointed to half empty plates. "He'll smell the food."

Lil sat at an empty table. "Good point." She knew Aimée would be right behind that dog. "Can you get some cooked meat? We can set it down as bait. By the way, what's your name?"

"Giselle. I'll be right back." Giselle returned with a plate of sliced chicken and sat. "I'll wait with you; he might remember me."

"Don't you have to go work?"

"I'm off now. I'd like to help." Her dimples deepened. "I'm bored silly working on this ship. By the way, where are you headed? After Dublin, that is."

Lil was saved from answering as two playful, yapping dogs bounced into the room, stopped, then ran to the food, arguing over who should get it.

Aimée came running in behind them. "*Mon Dieu*," she said out of breath. "These two took me all over this ship."

"Did you find their go-to spot?" Lil asked sarcastically.

"*Non*. We ran the entire time."

Lil stood. "We have to get back before Gustav finds us gone."

"Who's Gustav?" Giselle asked, suspiciously.

Aimée pulled a pout. "He's our bodyguard. Apparently, bad people are looking for us."

Lil grabbed Aimée's arm and squeezed. Hard. Shut up! she thought.

Giselle's head swiveled around. "Bad people?" Her interest perked up. "Tell me what they look like, and maybe I can find them. I'm all around this ship, in and out of rooms, too."

Aimée picked up Shamrock. "We don't know what they ..."

Lil pulled Aimée toward the door. "We have to go," she said. "Thanks for your help."

"All right," Giselle said. "Where are you headed, then? I'll get in touch if I notice anything strange."

"A friend's house in—" Aimée began.

Lil pulled her onto the staircase. "What's the matter with you?"

"She wants to help," Aimée said. "She's nice."

"Maybe," Lil said, hurrying her. "But Gustav said not to trust anyone. Remember?" She knocked on the suite door and it opened it immediately. Charlotte pulled them in as if she'd been standing there the entire time. "What happened? We were worried!"

Lil closed the door and turned the lock. "Has Gustav come by?"

"No, but it's almost eight. He'll be here any minute. Do we tell him?"

Aimée frowned. "No. We don't."

The girls glanced at each other, unsure.

"Come on. Nothing happened, did it? And here we are, back safely." Aimée let the dog drop and, fully tuckered out, he raced to his new bed, the pillow in the tub.

Charlotte turned to Juliette. "You're her sister. What do we do?"

The practical twin knew it wasn't helpful to save her sister every time she messed up, but telling would worry Gustav even more. "I think we should vote on it."

"Okay, we vote," Lil said. "But for the record, Aimée, you're one of the most frustrating, reckless people I know. This is the last time we save you." She let her black marble eyes bore into Aimée's for good measure. "Now. Everyone in favor of not telling."

Each girl raised her hand, but weakly.

"We won't stick up for you again," Lil said.

Gustav pulled the listening device from his ears. He wasn't grinning about that twin sister now. He would make his hourly check-in, then search for this person—this Giselle.

~

The next fourteen hours of cruising to Dublin went smoothly with no new calamities. Although there was one surprise yet to come.

The girls slept, read, played on their phones, and enjoyed board games. More word clues were gathered from the Ouija board, but those didn't make sense either. Meals came, and the dog was picked up for walks. Not by Giselle.

When the boredom had become nearly unbearable, a knock sounded and Gustav stepped inside. "Are you packed and ready? We dock in fifteen minutes."

"Yes, we are," Charlotte said. Each girl stood next to her luggage, and Charlotte held the dog. It had a leash now, securely wrapped around her wrist. This dog was going nowhere.

"Good. Let's go down to the ramp," Gustav said. "A car is waiting to drive us to Kenmare, generously provided by your father, Kalin. It's about a five-hour drive, without traffic."

"*Mon Dieu*," Aimée lamented. "Will this dreary trip never end? Before we leave, I want to stop by the kitchen and say good-bye to Giselle."

Gustav stiffened. "There is no one on this ship named Giselle."

"But we met—"

Gustav gave Aimée a look that said the conversation was over.

Aimée and Lil exchanged puzzled glances. What? No Giselle? She'd been real enough to them. Another riddle pressed down like a hundred-pound weight.

First the rogues on the train who almost kidnapped Aimée. Then the mysterious note, the pushy woman on the train, and now this disappearing woman. It would be five more hours before their next caper even began, and they already had more puzzles than clues. Way more.

Were they completely out of their league this time?

Chapter 23

The Stranger

As twilight shrouded the village of Kenmare, a fellow bent over a cane trudged slowly down the main street. His feet hurt especially bad. Even more than his hollow stomach. Villagers glared and then looked away, wondering where he lived. Such a poor creature who obviously had nothing. Homelessness had grown worse all around Ireland, including small villages like this one.

Unshaven and holding a ragged blanket like a shawl, the man skulked behind Crowley's Bar and hid between two large trash bins. His goal was to watch for members of the Corky gang who often slipped into the bar through the back door. Corkys were scoundrels who did the dirty work for underground markets headquartered in larger towns.

The castaway was waiting for one person in particular. Hearing sounds, he slipped more deeply into the shadows. Sure enough, there was Chester heading in for a pint.

A deep, foghorn voice penetrated the night. "How many casks d'ya have now?"

Chester turned to see three figures standing in the dim. He paled. "Near to fifty," he said, shakily. The deep voice belonged to Archibald, a Corky standing solid with two others, blocking the way to the bar. Any one of the three could crush him like a bunch of grapes.

Archibald scowled. "Fifty, is all? Can't get attention from the top with the likes of a pittance like that."

"Ain't easy to pull casks out of the rack house without getting caught," Chester said. "The old man watches like a hawk. He's got the nose for it too." He snorted at his own joke. No one laughed.

"Tell me," Archibald said. "How you doin' it? Pullin' off vats with no one knowing."

Chester spit out a stream of tobacco juice. "If I told ya that, I wouldn't have much leverage now, would I?" He wasn't about to tell the man he had a helper, his cousin Dickie, who would sell his soul for a pint of beer.

Archibald smiled, like a snake might smile. "Clever one, aren't ya? When you reach seventy barrels, we'll talk again. And what about the redheaded sister? She seen ya, right?"

"Her da sent her to some Frenchie school. She's long gone and won't be a problem."

The Corky boss looked knowingly at the woman next to him. "Are you sure about that, Chester? We heard otherwise, right, Giselle?" Archibald went on. "If that sister of his were to turn witness against you, you'd be no good to us anymore. Ya got that, mate?"

Chester shrugged as if unconcerned but swallowed hard. It was true that Finn's half-pint sister could become a problem. She'd seen him clear as glass that day at the dock. Otherwise, it was a perfect crime.

Archibald pulled a white handkerchief from his suit jacket and blew his egg-shaped nose. Then he folded the cloth neatly and shoved it back into a pocket. His lips lifted menacingly showing a silver tooth. "Meanwhile, my friend, you're buyin' us all a pint. Right, chaps?"

"Right, boss," the two said, lifting Chester by the arms, and carrying him into Crowley's bar.

When the pub door slammed shut, the blanketed man stepped out of his hiding place and made his way back to the ruins at Muckross Abbey. Pain stabbed with every step. By the time he leaned against the crumbling wall near his tunnel opening, it was fully dark. He had to choose these trips wisely; they took too much out of him. Hearing a sound, he looked upward to see a massive bird swooping toward him. It circled, then flew off. Plunk. Something heavy landed. He shuffled to it and saw a package wrapped in linen cloth, tied with twine. The vagabond held it to his chest. This would be the second one. Tears of gratitude rolled down his unshaven face.

The bird circled the towering stones, let out a shriek, then disappeared into the night. The recluse shook his head in wonder as he vanished into a dark tunnel of Muckross Abbey.

Chapter 24

Comrade-in-Arms

The day remained dull and gray as Gustav drove the girls the final stretch from Dublin, along the Ring of Kerry road to Kalin's summer home in Kenmare. They stared at the never-ending sea, mesmerized by long formations of waves, tall enough to devour the ship of an unskilled sailor. Seagoing vessels were rare in winter on the west coast, and for good reason. A purple-edged twilight formed over the horizon, as if trying to calm the waters.

Charlotte pulled her jacket more tightly around her. "I've never seen anything like this insane wind and crazy ocean." She looked out the other window and saw endless crisscross sections of rock walls marking off pasturelands. "So different. But where are all the people?"

Kalin laughed. "Not many here this time of year. Fishermen and a few shopkeepers is all. Who's left are folks with no money to escape the roughest months. They just batten everything down." She turned to Gustav, "Turn in here," she said, pointing up a rising, dirt road. "There's the homestead, right there at the top."

Four curious heads turned to the front windshield, taking in the lonely four-story house made from the same charcoal-gray rocks strewn about the landscape. The house looked as old as time, but improvements had been made: new windows all around, and a freshly painted porch. Stone chimneys stood tall and straight at each end, smoke billowing from both. The only trees were evergreens here and there, low to the ground and all leaning in one direction.

"A happy sight that chimney fume," Kalin said. "Means our housekeeper agreed to open the house for us, and cook. It'll be warm, at least."

"Will your parents be here?" Aimée asked, rubbing Shamrock's head as the limp pup nodded in and out of sleep.

"Off and on. Mum works in Killarney where our regular house is, and Da's in the distillery there, much of the time. But we'll have Mrs. Macready." Her smile turned mischievous. "You think Mother Weed's tough. Wait till you meet her. And of course, we have Gustav." She wondered how the two would get along.

Half listening, Gustav stared forward straight ahead, wondering what new calamities this girl-crew would bring. True, they weren't all reckless, but he'd have to stay on his toes. Each was notorious in her own way. Teenagers were a challenge, but five? And now they were deep in scoundrel territory. On two occasions, he believed their car was being followed, but the vehicles in question had veered off.

Gustav pulled the dusty black Suburban onto the stone drive before the house. The girls jumped out and, talking all at once, hauled their luggage out of the back.

Aimée dropped the dog, and it ran to the cliff's edge. As she grabbed the little thing's collar, goosebumps of fright prickled her neck as she looked down onto thunderous, crashing waves.

Lil followed, hollering over the deafening wind. "What a view! Like something out of a storybook." She caught her hat. "An Irish Gothic Fairy Story."

"There actually is a book called that," Juliette said, inching forward.

Lil scowled. "I know. I wasn't making it up."

"Let's go inside," Kalin said. "Best not to get too close to the edge with this wind."

"No kidding," Charlotte said, leaning back from a safer distance.

A gust swallowed her words as the door popped open and a tall woman appeared inside the frame. She stood solid as a ship's mast, wind sending strands of hair flailing around her head like thin, copper wires run amuck. Her long woolen skirt flapped around leather boots, well-worn but polished to a sheen.

"Oof!" the woman exclaimed as Shamrock darted between her legs and into the house. "Don't make me hold this door open all day, young'uns," she squawked in greeting. "We've got thirteen rooms to keep warm. Hello, wee Kalin. Good to see ya, lass. Get yer friends in here fast. It's colder than Hades out there."

"Yes, ma'am," Kalin said, and sent her comrades a knowing wink.

Everyone piled into the hallway like a flock of raucous birds. Beneath the center staircase, bags of all sizes and shapes filled the tiny space.

"Are ya movin' in, now?" Mrs. Macready asked. She gave Gustav a look of reproach. "Don't mar those walls young man, ye hear?" He quickly pulled his bags away from the newly polished tongue-and-groove paneling.

"Kalin, lass ... we're puttin' all of you—and this creature too, where'd he come from?—up in the big room on the fourth floor. Timothy helped me set up extra beds, dormitory style. That way all the noise will be in one place. Far away."

Kalin grinned and said, "This should be fun, bunking together." The twins and Charlotte nodded happily, but Lil frowned, annoyed by the woman's bossiness. The mothers were much nicer.

Mrs. Macready picked up a nearby broom and swept up the leaves and twigs flying around everyone's feet. "Up ya go now," she said, directing them upwards with long sweeps. Then she turned to Gustav, "You, sir, wait here."

The entourage stumbled up the carpeted steps behind Kalin, toward the fourth floor. Shamrock followed. The housekeeper watched them go, and when they were out of sight, she set her no-nonsense expression on the bodyguard who, from habit, snapped to attention as if facing his general assessing him for duty.

"You must be Gustav, the gent that our sire employed to keep the girls safe."

Gustav offered a snappy nod. "*Oui, madame.*"

"How sure are you of your assignment?"

Gustav lifted a single eyebrow. "What do you mean, *madame*?"

156

She drew up her chest. "Everyone one of my six brothers were in the Reserve Defense Forces. By an accident of birth, I wasn't allowed in, and by the time women were, I was too old. But that doesn't mean I didn't learn from the boys. I've cared for Kalin and her brother since they were babes. So, don't mess with me, young man. If anything happens to our wee Kalin, you'll answer to me ... and to me brothers."

Gustav wanted to pull off his fake glasses and tweed blazer, and posture up in his former ranger uniform, but instead he nodded gravely. "Do not worry, *madame*, I'll do my utmost to keep them all safe." Then on a hunch, he leaned forward, drawing her in. "May I depend on you? I'm new to this area and would most appreciate having an associate for this mission."

Mrs. Macready's lines of displeasure shifted to ones of intrigue. "Well, then, happy to assist. In fact, that would do nicely." Her demeanor held a hidden smile. "'Twill be our wee secret," she whispered, then opened the door on the left. "From this here room, you will see and hear all comings and goings. There's no other way out from the fourth floor."

Gustav grinned. "You seem to know these girls well, *madame*."

One corner of her mouth turned up, a rare thing. "I was young once, and livin' here in the wild west with six brothers, I learned a thing or two." Pointing him into the room, she eyed the odd-looking case as he laid it on the bed, but said nothing. "Dinner's at six, in two hours. Don't be late." She shut the guest room door firmly.

Gustav unpacked slowly, thinking about who might want Kalin so badly, and why. Someone had gone to a lot of trouble planting those men on the train, and the woman on the ship. Not sure how available Kalin's father, "the sire," would be, he was relieved to have a compatriot right here in the house. One you wanted with you, not against you. And she comes with well-trained brothers. This will do, he thought as his pulse slowly returned to normal. It will do nicely.

Chapter 25

The Summons

The girls and Gustav showed up to dinner at precisely six o'clock as ordered by Mrs. Macready. No one wanted to start off on the wrong foot. And sure enough, at the top of the hour, she stood like a field marshal near the swinging door to the kitchen. Offering a satisfied cluck and a nod at her obedient diners, she pushed open the door. "Come along, Timothy. We won't take all night now, will we?"

Scents of fresh baked bread filled the dining room as an enthusiastic young man with hair the color of rust falling over his eyes carried baskets and set them on the table. "Butter's 'ere," he said, pointing to two large tubs. "Right from Mr. MacIntosh's favorite Kerry cow." He whistled as he swung through the door, reappearing with a huge pot of fish chowder. With a jolly demeanor, in sharp contrast to his sister's stern one, he winked. "This'll warm yer bones for the long night." Using an enormous ladle, he filled the bowls that were passed down one by one.

"Will you join us?" Gustav asked.

Timothy looked hopeful, but his sister answered, "No, no. Not the likes of us. We'll have our fill after you're done. Oh, and the sire sent a note." She rummaged through a big pocket of her well-worn apron. "Here 'tis," she said, handing it to Gustav, who slit open the envelope and read:

Gustav,

Come to the distillery tomorrow at ten. I wish to speak to you and will give you a tour of our ancient, but still operating, house of spirits—of another kind. Heh, heh. Bring the girls, of course. I expect you to keep them with you, and out of danger, at all times.

Yours,

Declan

Gustav pocketed the note.

"What is it?" Kalin asked.

"We've been invited by your father to tour the distillery at ten tomorrow morning. We'll leave at nine fifteen to be certain." He set his steely eyes on them. "Be ready at the front door."

Dinner ended quickly, everyone lost in his or her own thoughts. The apple cake with custard sauce disappeared as if a genie had waved a wand when Kalin stood to leave.

"What about tea?" Mrs. Macready inquired in astonishment, as if no one ever left the table without at least a sip from her especially brewed leaves.

"We'll take mugs to our room," Kalin said, faking a yawn. "We're kind of tired."

"All right, lass. Come into the kitchen then and get your mugs filled."

With steaming cups in hand, the girls followed Kalin up the stairs to their room on the fourth. "Close the door," Kalin said to Lil, the last one in.

"What's up?" Lil said. "I'm not tired. It's only seven thirty."

"I know. But there's something I want to show you after Mrs. Macready and Timothy leave for home." She walked to the window overlooking the cobblestone drive. "We'll see them from here."

Lil joined her at the window and stared down forty feet to the scrub brush terrain below, dotted with these unusual Irish rocks. "You know, Kalin.

I'm not comfortable up here with only one way out. At the Abbey, at least I can drop down from my balcony in a pinch."

From their beds, Charlotte and the twins nodded in worried agreement.

"I know how to fix that," Kalin sipped her tea and said no more. A half hour passed and she perked up. "Look, they're leaving."

"I give up," Lil said. "What's the big mystery?"

Kalin skipped to the back of the long room, stopping at the brick chimney that cut through the ceiling. Impishly, she curled a finger for them to come. Then she knelt down, pulled back the corner of a straw mat, and pointed to a ring handle. She pulled. "This is how we get out without being seen, by this old staircase that got blocked off years ago. Finn showed me in case I ever needed to escape."

"Do your parents know?" Charlotte asked.

"They do, but Mrs. Macready doesn't. At the bottom, the door leads into a shed she never goes into. Finn keeps fishing rods, bait, and guy stuff there. It's locked from the outside."

"Let's go," Lil said. "I want to see where it comes out."

"Me too," Aimée said, jumping off the bed. Then she looked dubiously at the bedroom door. "Are you sure Gustav won't know?"

"Never. His room is at the front of the house. This passageway comes out in the back. We'll have to be quiet on the steps though." She opened a large cedar chest. "We'll need light."

Reluctantly, Charlotte accepted a flashlight. "Why do we want to sidestep our body guard? He's here to protect us, right?"

"We're not sidestepping him," Lil said. "We're just discovering alternatives, for safety. Like in a fire. And besides, the little mutt probably needs to … you know." The dog whined.

Juliette stretched out. "I don't mind staying here."

"We all should go," Kalin said. "So we know the way." Her face turned secretive. "Finn used these stairs to meet his chailin … his girlfriend."

Flashlight in hand, Kalin led the way down the narrow, curving stairs that ran directly behind the chimney, where the smells of dinner lingered from the wood cookstove.

Lil stopped to shine her light upwards. She gulped. Spiders hung provocatively at every turn. "Keep your light down," she said, remembering that Charlotte was terrified of arachnids.

Finally they stood, crushed one behind the other, on the bottom steps. Kalin put her ear to the door and, hearing nothing but the howling wind, turned the knob. "Wait here." She disappeared into blackness. A light flicked on, and she waved everyone into a stone hut smelling of dirt and fish bait. Wind whistled through holes in the walls.

Aimée pinched her nose shut. "Gross!"

Lil looked out the dirty glass pane. "I want to go outside."

"Okay, but not too far. The cliff. Remember?"

Charlotte lingered as they stepped out into the wind. "Are you sure Gustav can't see us?"

"Not unless he's outside right now. I'll go first and look around." Kalin disappeared into the night, and then waved her light for the others to come.

Flashlight beams lit up the grounds as they wandered the yard, toward the cliff and the roaring sea. Lil walked to the edge and looked down. "What's down there?"

"A rocky beach," Kalin said from behind her. "We'll go tomorrow. There's a path we can follow to the bottom."

Abruptly, Lil spun around. "Brrr, too cold. Let's go back in."

Shivering, the girls followed her to the stone shed. As they relocked the door and climbed the stairs, Lil felt torn in half. She'd just seen something suspicious on the beach below. Two fiery lights, like lit cigarettes, moving in the blackness. Someone was down there. Should she tell, or would that worry everyone? Kalin was being followed, all right. But by whom? And how did they know she was back?

Chapter 26

The Waterwheel

The next morning, a tired Gustav and the girl detective team piled into the car for the drive to Killarney. No one had slept well. The wind—that raucous night goblin—had tried its best to get inside their stone house on the hill. Even now the car pitched and pulled, buffeted by the gales. Forbidding storm clouds raced across the sky.

Gustav glanced at Kalin, dozing off in the front seat. "I need directions, young lady."

She perked up. "Yes, sir. And sorry for the wind. It's always worse in winter."

"You, *chérie*, are not responsible for Mother Nature. Just keep me on the correct road to the distillery. *Oui?*"

Swaying motions lulled the sleepy girls, except Kalin, who had to pay attention and offer directions. But the trip was too quick for a solid nap, and soon Gustav turned onto the road that led to the three-hundred-year-old distillery, distinctive with its tall, brick smokestack.

As they pulled up in front of a building that sat at the edge of a waterway, Kalin's father emerged wearing gloves and a leather apron over work clothes. He and Gustav shook hands. "Excuse my appearance. Been fussing with the waterwheel. Always needing repairs, that one."

Gustav's eyebrow rose. "I look forward to seeing it, *monsieur*. I understand it's original."

"'Tis, at that. You're welcome to see all. Come to Da, Kalin. Looks like these girls have been good for you." Sighing, he folded her into a fatherly hug.

The group stepped into a bright room decorated with memorabilia from centuries of grain fermentation: a wall-mounted half barrel with the company's fancy logo, bulbous pottery stills connected to odd-shaped lengths of tubing. One corner of the room held a bar for tasting, something the girls would not do. Gustav, however might be enticed into a sip. Although he preferred French brandy, which he found far superior to whiskey.

Declan waved the group forward. "We'll start our tour with what everyone wants to see, the water-wheel, where she's been for nearly three hundred years." He led them to an outside platform adjacent to the gargantuan wheel, partially visible above a fast-moving stream. Wide, wooden panels were covered in moss and stood perfectly still.

"We stop her when we make repairs," Declan said. "Her job is the most important one in the distillery. When in motion, the wheel paddles the water that turns the machinery inside. We run the business much like the old timers did," he added with a sense of pride. His arms moved like a conductor's, pointing out an array of massive and confusing equipment.

Instead of leaning over the canal to inspect the wheel, Lil stayed inside. She preferred to explore on her own, rooms that housed huge copper tubs and barrel casks. She recognized the rack house, where the maturing liquid would rest inside casks for years. Gazing up at barrels stacked to the ceiling, she wondered how they got way up there. Then voices forced her into the shadows as two men entered the room. One looked familiar.

"Chester, I'm takin' you off night shift," the heavier man said.

Chester, looked startled. "Why is that?"

"You have to ask the old man. I'm just passin' on orders."

Visibly agitated, Chester asked, "When does that start?"

"Next week."

"Is that why you called me in early? You coulda told me tonight."

"Yeah, well, Mr. D needs help with the waterwheel just now. Go on out back before they dock your paycheck for lost distilling time."

Chester frowned deeply and stomped out to the wheel. When the other man left the room, Lil stepped out from her hiding spot. Goosebumps ran up and down her arms. This was the same man Madame Villars's image had shown them. Chester! The man with horrible teeth, who had run away on the dock. And he's here. Another clue, directly in front of her.

She heard her name being called and headed toward the sound. The tour group had stepped into the mash room where water and grains got mixed together.

Kalin's forehead creased. "Where have you been?" she whispered.

"Oh, sorry, got sidetracked."

"Da says to stay together; these machines can be risky."

"Where is he now, your da?"

Kalin pointed to the back. "He had to go meet with someone who's fixing a broken paddlewheel. We're to wait here till he gets back. Gustav's with them."

"Did you see him? The fixit man?"

"No. Why?" Kalin asked, then turned as her father and Gustav returned.

"Tell you later," Lil whispered.

"Now," Declan said, taking control of the tour. "On the next steps in the process ..."

The girls sighed; this wasn't how they'd imagined their trip to Ireland would be. Yes, the waterwheel was cool, and the room-sized steam engine beyond belief, like a mechanical dragon. But making whiskey wasn't exactly exciting. Still, they politely followed Declan from room to room, not remembering a single word he said.

Chester puffed nervously on the lit cigarette sticking out of his mouth. His hands shook as he hung out over the rush of water, cutting away rotten pieces of paddle wood needing replacement. His mind wasn't on his work. All he could think was Finn's sister—she was here, inside the distillery. And only by the luck of the clover she hadn't see him. He prayed the old man wouldn't bring them out here. If she saw his face, it would be all over. He'd be arrested, but not before the Corkys had their way with him. They seemed to know everything before he did.

Suddenly the wheel shook violently and Chester leaned backwards, falling safely onto the platform. Shaking like the weak leaf he was, he pulled himself up onto rubbery legs. Then he leaned out again to make sure the wheel had stabilized before returning to his repair job.

He let out a series of curses that will not be repeated here. This old relic will be the death of someone yet, he thought.

Chapter 27

That Boy Knew Something

Lil fidgeted all the way back to the stone house. She could barely wait to tell the team she'd just seen Finn's killer. But not in front of Gustav. This new clue was outrageously solid. The actual villain practically living under their noses. She closed her eyes, trying to be patient.

Meanwhile, Gustav considered his own theories. While at the distillery, Declan had filled him in on his son's disappearance. That's what the police had called it, a disappearance, not a murder. They believed he'd run away because he hated working in the distillery. But Declan swore his son would never have left without a word to his mother or his sister.

Declan said Kalin had seen the explosion— adding that her visions always proved true. The police did find burnt wood from his boat, but no body after four months. Before Finn's death, Declan had suspected someone was stealing. Had Finn found out and been killed for it? If so, why hadn't he shared his own doubts with his father? Gustav was drawn in to the mystery and wanted to solve it. He would talk to the housekeeper and her brothers and ask what they knew. The girls were definitely in danger and could never go out on their own. Threats had grown daily, first on the train, then on the ship, and now right here in Kenmare.

A sudden storm kicked up. Great pelts of rain blew onto the windshield, making it hard to see, even with wipers flying fast. He'd ponder the mystery later.

After the car arrived, the group scurried inside. Delicious smells teased their empty stomachs. Five hungry girls followed the aroma to the kitchen, to the ire of Mrs. Macready.

"Did you young-uns take off your wet boots? And lunch ain't ready yet." Her face shone with perspiration as she bent over the double oven pulling out four crusty loaves of honey oat bread. Then, like a juggler, she switched from potholder to wooden spoon to stir a steaming kettle of potato leek soup.

"We're starving!" Kalin said, and grabbed a smaller spoon to dip, irresistibly, into the buttery broth. Her tummy growled like an exclamation point.

Mrs. Macready snatched the spoon from her hand. "Go on up to your rooms. I'll call once everything's ready."

Kalin faced her longtime nanny with a well-rehearsed pout. The others waited to see how good she was at swaying the woman. But Mrs. Macready rose up like a periscope fixing on its target. She stared down at Kalin and then gave each girl a meaningful look. It wasn't a wacky, unpredictable expression like Mother Weed's. It was a glare that would melt the spine of any adversary. "And take this shaggy thing you call a dog upstairs with you," she added. He's been a whiny nuisance all day, chasing the cats all 'round." Shamrock barked as if in agreement.

Giving up, Kalin picked up Shamrock and sighed. "Come on, girls. No use arguing."

"Now you've got the way of it, lass," the housekeeper said, and turned back to the soup.

Once in their room, Lil let out a rumbling breath she'd been holding all the way home. She walked to the window and perused the cliff's edge through the deluge of rain.

"Lil, what is it?" Juliette asked. She had felt her own inklings while at the distillery.

Aimée joined her at the window. "Tell us."

"You're not going to believe this," Lil said. "Remember the insanely creepy guy we saw in Madame Villars's waterfall? I saw him during the distillery tour. His name is Chester."

"What?" everyone yelled together.

Charlotte asked, "Are you sure?"

"Absolutely. I'd never forget that horrible face."

Kalin's own face turned icy white, and she plopped down on her bed. "Damnaigh! Things are starting to make some sense."

"They are," Lil said. "And the other thing is, while we were outside last night, I saw lights moving around at the bottom of the cliff. Like cigarette smokers down there, keeping an eye on the house. We need to go over our clues."

Aimée rubbed her hands together. "Now we're getting somewhere. One of us should go down to the beach tonight. Sneak up on them and eavesdrop."

Lil and Juliette argued against the idea. Her most ludicrous yet.

Holding tight to the talisman, Charlotte said, "No one should be going to the beach. Don't you get it, Aimée? These are real killers."

"But," Aimée protested, "don't we have to know their plan? How else do we catch them?"

"We create our own, better plan, and then we get them. Tell us more, Lil."

Lil cleared her throat. "Like I said ..."

She was interrupted by pounding on the door. Then a voice, "Are you girls coming down to lunch? I've been hollering myself into laryngitis. And it won't do me to get sick. Not with you all needin' me." Grumbles about her poor legs trailed off as she descended to the kitchen.

"Looks like we go eat first," Lil acknowledged.

Juliette walked to the door. "We'll all be smarter after a good meal."

Lil took a final glance out the window and saw Gustav standing at the cliff's edge, peering down. He knows, she thought. Our bodyguard knows this place is being watched.

The rain had stopped, giving Gustav a chance to scope out the cliffside. He looked down thirty feet and watched giant waves crash onto the rocky shore. The roaring sound erased everything, even the wind. No one down there with this high tide, he thought, and he turned back.

Catching movement, he looked up to see Lil walking away from the window. Always looking, that one. He supposed he'd have to bring her in sooner or later. All of them, really. He knew they considered themselves detectives of a sort, which could be more trouble than it was worth. How to keep them at home? Maybe give them an assignment to keep them out of harm's way.

A fast wall of fog moved toward him, and he walked to the porch. The housekeeper stepped outside, a shawl anchoring her windswept hair. "Where are the girls?" Gustav asked.

"Eating lunch. I heard them say they wanted to go to their room after, to play some game. Weegee, or some such."

Gustav grinned knowingly. The Ouija board. He'd heard them playing it on the ship, looking for clues. The silly game might actually be one way to keep them distracted. His smile disappeared. "Mrs. Macready, I want to meet with you and your brothers. I have questions about the town, about Finn." He bent his head, respectfully.

Mrs. Macready teared up. "That boy didn't just up and disappear, may the Lord bless his soul. I've known him since he was in diapers. Finn was here one minute, gone the next. No, sir. Someone got rid of him!"

"You mean killed?" Gustav asked.

"Yes, sir. That boy knew something!"

She turned to the door. "I'll bring the brothers to you tonight."

Chapter 28

The Three Bs

After dinner, Gustav sat at a small desk and made a list of everything he knew. He needed to plan his next move. Although he'd been hired as a bodyguard for the girls, the mystery of Finn's murder was too compelling to ignore. Somehow the two were tied together—the explosion and why the girls were here. Coming to Ireland to write a story was a ruse—a cover-up. He had yet to see a single girl with pen and paper except to write down clues for some vague reason.

A knock sounded, and he opened the door. Mrs. Macready stood with three ginger-haired, young men behind her. "Here are three of 'em," she said waving her lanky brothers into the room. "The other two are busy tonight. Close the door," she ordered the tallest man.

Gustav shook hands as the housekeeper announced each odd name which he tried to memorize. But they looked so much alike, it was difficult to sort them out.

"So, ask away," Mrs. Macready said, not one for small talk.

Gustav cleared his throat. "Yes, well, I do have questions. Lots of them. But mostly I want to know this. Why was Finn at risk, and needed to be ... er ... eliminated?"

The tallest brother, Brin—or was it Breen?— spoke up. Gustav struggled to understand the strong Irish brogue. "Finn told us his worries about the distillery, like. Over the last year especially. We've all worked there at one time or other, helpin' out."

His sister glared at him. "Get to the point, Breen. This gentleman don't have all night."

Breen rolled his eyes, and before he had a chance to speak again, the shortest brother said "He were scared sure enough, Finn was. Right before he disappeared, he told us, all three of us—we're triplets, you see, and are together a lot. Finn ... he said he knew a certain one was stealin' whiskey. And he wanted to find where this cur was hidin' the barrels, and—"

The middle twin lost patience with his doppelganger, and jumped in. "Here's the simple truth of it. Finn was explorin' tunnels along the shoreline. He was bound to find the stash and impress his da. We think he did find them. And then, poof!" His arms made a circular motion.

Gustav removed his fake glasses and rubbed the bridge of his nose. His flinty eyes drilled into the men. "Did you talk to the police about this?"

Breen shook the broom-like hair away from face. "Yes, sir, we did. But they were convinced Finn ran away, so they paid us no mind. And us three ..." He glanced at his brothers, who nodded, egging him on. "We're pretty sure Finn is dead. None of us dares go look for the whiskey, or we be next."

"I see," Gustav said. "Someone's been watching this house from the beach below."

"Spot on, sir. We've seen men prowlin' about," the housekeeper said. "At first, we thought, the cops. But no. It's Corkys, we think. No idea why, the house being empty and all."

"Probably on the lookout for Kalin's return," Gustav said. The others grunted in agreement. "Which means they now know she's here."

The conversation went on longer, but nothing more was learned. Mrs. Macready yawned. "It's time for me beauty sleep so's I can get back here with the sun. Let's go, boys." As she left the room, she looked at Gustav. "We'll talk more on the morrow."

Gustav nodded solemnly. "Yes, ma'am. Tomorrow I'll give the girls an assignment to keep them inside the house. And I'll want to get a message to Declan."

"Good. Keep 'em busy and out of danger. I know what I'd be doin', and I don't trust 'em an inch." Mrs. Macready winked and closed the door to his room. After following her brothers down the porch steps, she stopped. "What was that?" she asked the dark.

"Huh?" they replied in unison.

The housekeeper waved an arm. "You boys go on. I'll be checkin' on something."

Never ones to question their elder sister and her seeings, the men nodded and strolled down the driveway, voices and bodies melting into the night. A flashlight beam guided them toward the fishing village at the bottom of the hill.

Mrs. Macready crept around the house to Finn's shed. She squinted and thought she saw the door slightly open. Rushing to it, she pulled. No, it was locked. A shuffling noise inspired her to peer in through the dirty glass. She felt more than saw something move, but nothing could be seen. Must be a critter routing around for bait. She hurried 'round to catch up with her brothers. Her imagination was having a bit of fun with her. No one's been in that shed since Finn went missing, and he had the only key. Still, she was left with a peculiar feeling.

Legs quivering, Lil rose from her crouch. She hadn't even blinked when that mouse scurried over her feet. At least she hoped it was a mouse, not a rat. But it was worth it; the nosy house-keeper hadn't seen her. It was safe to head up the stairs. Wait till I tell everyone what I overheard, she thought, using hands and feet to climb fast.

"Did you hear anything good?" Aimée asked as Lil tumbled in from the hatch.

"You're not going to believe this," Lil said excitedly.

"Tell us, quick," Kalin said. "I have to know why the B brothers were here."

"B brothers?"

"Mrs. Macready's brothers. We call them that because their names sound alike and all start with B. They're triplets."

Lil's eyes were lit like vintage marbles. "Gustav's window was cracked, so I heard everything. They're convinced Finn had been searching caves for the stolen barrels. That he was trying to catch the thief and find the whiskey to impress your father. We now know that Chester is the thief. And you're a witness, Kalin."

Everyone started talking at once.

"Hold on!" Charlotte shouted. They quieted. "We need a plan before we do anything foolish. Let's go over our clues and add what we just learned." She read their notes out loud.

Then Juliette put up a hand. "I've figured something out."

"What?" Her sister encouraged.

"Give her time," Lil said. "You know she has to ponder."

They waited as Juliette paced and pulled on her long, silvery braid. Finally, she stopped. "I've got it." Her voice was soft, and the girls leaned in. "This entire mystery revolves around the stolen casks, right? If we find those, we solve the mystery. I say we go to Muckross Abbey, sneak into those tunnels, and search. There must be a tunnel that runs from the Abbey all the way to the shore." She closed her eyes. "I see barrels stacked high." Her eyes opened. "Right after Lil saw Chester at the distillery, I had a vision that we'd found them."

Lil piped in. "You're right! We find the casks and show Declan where they are. Then Kalin will bear witness against Chester, and they'll arrest him. We'll have finished what Finn started."

No one spoke as they contemplated the risks of going into the tunnels alone.

Kalin said, "It might not be so easy. There are a few tunnels. We could get lost. Who would know where to look for us?"

Juliette said, "Think of the Ouija clue words, tide and fish. We saw Chester unloading barrels on a beach, near the shore. We find a tunnel that runs all the way from the ruins to the shore. How many of those could there be? That's where the casks will be."

"But," Aimée broke in. "What about the clue word ... Corkys? They're the bad guys. What if they find us first?"

"Even if they do," Lil said. "I doubt they'd kill five teenagers. It would invite the police to dig deeper. And they'd have Gustav on them. Not even the police would mess with him."

Charlotte said, "The clues point to a tunnel at the ruins, and a tunnel at the shoreline. I agree there must be one that connects both places. The Corkys' written note to those dweebs on the train instructed them to take Kalin to a tunnel at the ruins." Suddenly, her chest felt warm and she grabbed hold of the medallion. "Look. This thing is heating up."

All eyes went to the sigil hanging around Charlotte's neck, the gift from Madame Villars. Now it was glowing crimson. "This is going to guide us to the barrels," she said.

Aimée jumped up. "Our next adventure! We should leave before the sun comes up."

Chapter 29

A Surprise in the Tunnel

At four-thirty the next morning, Charlotte's phone played a bugle tune, and she leapt up like the house was on fire. Then she took in a relaxing breath. Oh, the tunnels. "Everyone," she whispered loudly, "Wake up."

"We are awake," Aimée grumbled. "Who could sleep through that?"

"And make sure you dress warm," Charlotte added, reaching for her pile of clothes.

"We know," Aimée whined. She preferred getting up with the sun, not before it.

Lil pulled up her jeans. "She just wants us to be safe. Let's not start off arguing."

187

They quickly dressed and slid on their pre-filled backpacks. Food and water Kalin liberated from the kitchen had been divided equally among them.

"I hope we have enough," Aimée said. "We don't know how long we'll be down there."

"You won't starve," Juliette said. "This trip has given you a little extra fat to burn."

Aimée scowled. "If we weren't prisoners, I'd get more exercise."

It went on like that. But even though they preferred cozy, warm beds, they were dressed within minutes.

Charlotte stood near the lifted hatch. "Ready, ladies? Remember, no talking till we get to the ruins. It'll be sunrise in twenty minutes. Does everyone have their flashlight ready? Good. Whoever is last, pull down the cover." Then she disappeared down the staircase.

Kalin was last to descend and she dutifully lowered the hatch with a silent prayer to find the stolen barrels. The hatch snapped into place. However, no one had thought about the mat that hid the trap door.

As the detective team approached the crumbling walls and fallen spires of the Abbey ruins, the sun inched up the horizon. Reds and oranges lit up the enormous stones standing in a circle. A tribute to some ancient religion. Spits of coral fog chased away the night shadows.

"This is so cool," Lil said, craning a look at the tallest vertical rock. "I've always wanted to see one of these Stonehenge things. How did they get here, anyway?"

Charlotte looked at her timepiece. "Later. Now we look for tunnel openings." They spread out among the ruins and after five minutes, Charlotte called, "Over here! The medallion's warming up!"

The girls joined her at the mouth of a super large shaft bounded by a moss-covered, stone-and-dirt wall. Muddy water dripped down the rocks, exuding a musty odor. The girls squinted into the dark opening. It was one thing to imagine, quite another to actually enter this repulsive place.

"The medallion says this is the right one," Charlotte encouraged.

"We have to go in, or this trip is for nothing," Kalin said.

Charlotte and Kalin took a few steps into the gloom, noses bombarded with cold and damp. The medallion heated up even more. "This is definitely it," Charlotte said. "Let's go."

The others followed her inside.

No one noticed the giant bird perched on the tallest stone of the great stone circle.

∾

The stranger's body was racked with a bone-shaking shiver as he sat in the near-dark, poking his dwindling campfire. He couldn't get warm anymore, no matter how much wood he burned. And now he'd taken to talking out loud. "You're dying, man," he told himself, morosely. Salty tears dribbled into his straggly beard, tickling his chin. "You've gotta do something different. But what to do? What to do?"

Like a lost child, he glared at the wall, hoping it might have an answer. The wall blurred but didn't speak, although he would not have been surprised if it had, given he was half crazy. He groaned himself upright and steadied weak legs with help from his stick. Pulling the scruffy blanket more firmly around him, he set off stumbling down the tunnel. "The bird. Must find that bird. Then ... talk ... to someone. Get help, 'fore it's too late and I meet my maker."

After shuffling along, all bumble-footed, he heard voices. Angels' voices, in lilting echoes.

Like music, like siren songs at sea. Or maybe he was dead and didn't realize it. He groaned. No. Still too much pain to be dead.

The sounds quieted and he dragged himself on. "Don't tell me I can't do this," he yelled at the walls, then started a yelling rampage. "I will make it ... make it. I will make it ... make it." His voice and echoes, hoarse yet fearsome, peeled loudly down the passageway.

"Stop!" Charlotte exclaimed, arms out. "Did you hear that?"

"Yeah," Lil said, and moved closer to the sound. "Shh!"

Listening intently, the girls heard a voice—definitely a man's voice. Something about making it, making it, over and over.

"Someone's down here," Lil whispered.

"What if it's one of the Corkys?" Aimée said. "Guarding the barrels."

"Doubtful. We're not close to shore yet," Kalin said. "That's probably a half mile down."

"Who could it be, then?" Aimée asked.

Juliette felt goose bumps rush down her neck and spine, which preceded her visions. "Hold on. I see a man. He's trapped here. I think he needs our help."

"Maybe," Aimée said. "But he could be bad, too."

Kalin shone her light around and discovered a deep alcove in the tunnel wall. "Look, we can hide in there, and after he walks by, we'll decide whether or not to talk to him."

The man's voice got louder, sounding downright crazy. Frightened, the girls skittered into the alcove. "Lights off," was the last thing anyone said.

The raggedy, blanketed man stumbled past the hideout, babbling nonsense. He was bent over a crude walking stick that barely held him upright.

Suddenly, Kalin let out a sob, turned on her light, and rushed out of the alcove.

Aimée reached out. "Kalin. Wait!"

"I know that man," Kalin said, pushing away.

The man stopped short; tipping an ear to listen. Kalin aimed her light at him. "I know you," she called out. "It is you! You're my brother!"

The vagabond turned to her and dropped his stick. "Holy Mary, Mother of God," he said in a weak voice, dropping to the ground. "Kalin," he blubbered putting his hands to his head. "I'm dreaming, or I'm dead. Can this be my own ... my own sister, Kalin? Are we both dead?"

"No, Finn! You're alive. We're both alive!" She beamed the light over him then gasped. "But barely." Falling into his outstretched arms, she cried in loud gulping sobs.

Feeling pulses of shock and amazement, one by one, the girls wandered out of the alcove. Charlotte shone her light over the siblings as the team witnessed a most implausible reunion.

Finn, whom everyone had believed to be dead, was alive.

Chapter 30

Tricked Solid

Gustav poked at his fish and eggs, not his usual breakfast of croissants, strawberry jam, and expresso. He rubbed his temples, wondering how to approach the girls with the fake assignment Maybe they should write a trip report. For the parents, not the school. The Abbey was peculiar, something he would talk to Charlotte about in the future. Supposedly, the girls were here to write a story about Ireland—for a magazine. They certainly knew how to create cover stories. Perhaps they had a future in French intelligence?

His head snapped up as Mrs. Macready pushed through the swinging kitchen door. "Where are those lasses?" She eyed the covered bowls on the table. "Food's gettin' cold."

Gustav choked down a sip of weak, black coffee and stood. "I'll go upstairs and see." He'd do anything to get away from the smell of fish in the morning.

"Thank you, young man. You'll save these old legs going up four flights, you will." She turned to the kitchen. "I'll pour you a fresh cup when you get back."

Not wanting to offend, he offered a weak wave on his way to the front staircase. Once outside the bedroom, he put an ear to the door. How odd, no sound at all from that noisy pack. He knocked. Nothing. His heart kicked into overtime and he knocked louder. "Girls, breakfast awaits. It'll be a real favorite." Still no answer.

Something was wrong, very wrong. He twisted the knob and entered. "Hello? Ladies?" The room was empty. How in the world? He raced to each window. All locked. His head twisted and turned wildly as he searched for clues when he spotted a pile of rug. Running to it he saw the trap door. What's this? A secret exit? He grabbed the ring and pulled to see a hidden staircase. *Incroyable!*

Gustav spewed words that shall not be repeated here. He pulled a small emergency light from his pocket and bounded down the curving staircase, finding himself inside Finn's shed. The outside door was ajar. His stomach dropped, and his temples pulsed. He'd been tricked solid. More cursing propelled him around the house to the front door and to Mrs. Macready.

Seeing the look on Gustav's face as he stormed into the kitchen, hers paled. "They can't be gone, she cried, and leaned against the countertop. "I can't lose another one, I tell ye!"

"We'll find them. Call Declan and your brothers to set up a search. *Maintenant!*" His French flew fast and furious, scolding himself all the way to his room.

The housekeeper forced her legs to the phone. As in the old days, the house had a black instrument on a table in the hallway. She picked up the earpiece and dialed.

Used to gearing up for emergencies, Gustav pulled on a uniform of warm, dark clothing. He grabbed what he'd need for the search and stuffed everything into his backpack. The curious container was slung over his shoulder.

The housekeeper looked him up and down. She knew this was not his first search mission, but it was probably the first in a peaceful hamlet. "My brothers will be right along. She reached into a cabinet and pulled out a small bottle of brown liquid. "I'll just be needin' a bit of the grain," she said, and poured a dram into her feeble coffee.

Gustav admired her all the more. Mrs. Macready was as sturdy as they came, but even the strongest person can be weakened by the loss of a loved one.

Within minutes, the three Bs knocked on the door. Just shy of a half hour, Declan burst inside, red in the face and looking like he wanted to tear something apart.

He glared at Gustav. "You've lost 'em?" Then he held up his fists. "Why, I should—"

Gustav put up his palms. "Hold on. We can explain."

Finding her backbone, Mrs. Macready moved in between them and glared at Declan accusingly. "You, sir. You never told me about the other staircase. If we'd known, those rascals would still be here."

"What staircase?" Declan said, lowering his arms. Then the light dawned. "You mean the back stairs? Only Finn knew about those."

"Well, did ya think he might have told his sister about 'em, you goose?" the housekeeper asked, dripping sarcasm.

As the two bickered, Gustav jumped in. "Enough. We're losing time. Let's use it to figure out where they've gone."

Breen broke in. "Knowin' Kalin like I do, and that she's like 'er brother, I do believe she'd go on a search. For the missing casks. Show her da she's just as good as he."

Declan turned on the brothers. "What do you know about the casks, then?"

"Well, since you never asked us, we'll tell you anyway," Breen said. "That son of yours was searchin' for the stolen whiskey. Then he disappeared."

Gustav stopped pacing. "This is wasting time. Remember the note I showed you, Declan, from the train? It talked about the ruins, the tunnels. I say we start there. Search those tunnels. We might find both the girls and your barrels."

Declan ran trembling fingers through his hair. "But how will we know which tunnel? There's a riddle of them at the ruins."

Gustav tapped his molded case. "I've got something right here that'll help us."

Chapter 31

The Mysterious Case

Charlotte squatted down, close to the siblings who clung to each other. "Finn, I'm Charlotte, and I'm thrilled we found you but you need food ... right away."

Kalin wiped her tear-stained face with her sleeve. "Sorry, love. Finn, these are my best friends in the whole world. They've been helping me." She hugged him again. "Oh, Finn, there's so much to tell you. Yes, this is Charlotte. She's the daughter of a French duke and duchess, and she keeps us organized. Here's Lil, the best and bravest detective ever, and decipherer of clues." She stood and pulled the twins in to her. "And

Aimée and Juliette. Twins who couldn't be more different but each wonderful. They believed in me from the first. We came home to solve your disappearance, Finn, but this … this is a miracle I never expected!" New tears brimmed.

Finn grabbed his stick and stood shakily. "Can hardly believe it myself. Let's go to my campsite yonder down this cave. I daren't show my face outside."

"We understand," Charlotte said taking an arm. "Save your strength. We'll help you."

She and Lil, being the strongest two, held Finn up and gently walked him the distance to his hideout cave. They covered him with the few blankets he'd managed to find and pulled cheese, bread, and water from their packs.

"Don't eat too much, or too fast," Juliette said. "Here, drink this first."

He drained the water bottle in seconds. "Got sick on sea water," he said.

Aimée pulled out a few pieces of wood she'd taken from behind the house. "Don't look so shocked, everyone. Told you I was worried we'd get lost down here." They laughed.

"So, your annoying worries come in handy once in a while," Lil said.

"They argue like this all the time," Kalin said. "But they love each other."

Finn looked up from his cheese and cucumber sandwich, his face jubilant. "Whoever you are, to me you are angels sent from heaven." He swallowed hard. "Tell me what you know."

As Aimée added wood to a dwindling fire, Kalin filled her brother in on every detail. Her vision of the explosion, believing he was dead. And about Madame Villars, the Abbey, and the abbess and her cohorts, sending them to Ireland to solve the mystery. "These women are part of a sisterhood, like the old days, before everything changed."

Finn smiled through cracked lips. "I like the sound of that place, the Abbey. Reminds me of our ancestors."

"Exactly," Kalin said. "And Finn, we know who tried to kill you. Someone named Chester. He still works at the distillery. Lil saw him yesterday."

Finn's face reddened, and he shook his head, his crimson hair swinging in clumps. "He followed me, you know, and figured out I knew his secret. That day by my boat? I caught a whiff of something burning and dove just in time, kicking away. The frigid water protected me. Then I hid here, not far from the casks. One night, outside of Crowley's, I overheard the Corkys say they wanted more barrels. I think Chester plans to steal more."

"He usually works at night," Lil said. "But he's going on day shift next week. So, maybe he'll risk taking more, tonight."

Finn turned to her. "How'd you learn that?"

"I told you," Kalin said. "She's a great detective." Finn gave Lil an admiring smile.

"Well, this detective has a question. Why hide here like an animal? Why not just go to the village police with the evidence you found?"

"That's easy. Chester has a man inside the police department. My parents were living an hour away. I did sneak up to the summer house, but it was being watched by Corkys. I was trapped, all the way around."

Lil nodded and then smiled slyly. "Now, we'll trap the real rat."

∾

Gustav, Declan, and the triplets arrived at the ruins of Muckross Abbey. Columns of fog drifted up and around crumbling towers and lofty rock walls. Gustav examined several tunnel openings. Which one did those blasted girls go into? he wondered.

"Dunno," Breen said. "They could be lost in any one of 'em."

Gustav hadn't asked the question out loud. "Is everyone in Ireland telepathic?"

Declan scowled. "I'll telepathic you if anything happens to those girls."

"Yes, sir." Gustav opened his mysterious case. Time to bring on a bit of his own telepathic technology: high-tech tracking gear. He lifted out a flat processor made from a unique alloy and tapped a few side buttons on the unit. A jumble of wiry antennae rolled out.

"What in Hades is that?" Declan asked.

"Something we used in the Middle East to find lost people in caves. Human sensitivity radar, HSR. Reads people's electromagnetic fields. You never saw it, by the way."

The B brothers exchanged looks, thrilled to be in on an intelligence secret.

Holding the unit in front of him, Gustav took a few steps into each cavern. At the third one, the unit lit up like the Eiffel Tower at night. "This is it," he said grinning.

"Can that contraption find whiskey?" Declan asked.

Gustav laughed, an unusual occurrence. "When we find the girls, I have a feeling we'll find your missing barrels."

Chapter 32

Another Discovery

Back at his hideout, Finn watched the girls toss around ideas for catching Chester. They were so smart, so confident, not like any girls he knew. They made a good team. His sister was lucky.

Then they heard voices. Men's voices.

"Shh," Lil said, and tiptoed to the opening of the cave. She peered out and jumped back. "It's Gustav, with other men. Too dark to see who, but his face is lit up by a weird machine."

Juliette said, "It's whatever was in that strange case. It can sense us."

"Oh, no," Aimée whined. "They're going to find us. We don't want their help; we want to solve the mystery ourselves."

Finn looked at her in surprise. "You did solve it. You found the thief and you found me." He looked around at his dreadful surroundings. "I wouldn't have lasted much longer in this place." He stood up all wobbly, intent on getting home.

"Whoa," Charlotte said, and lowered him to his cocoon of pungent blankets. "Just a little longer, Finn. But you're right. We have to let ourselves be saved and get you home. I'll bet you can't wait for a good bath and a long sleep. We have to let Gustav help us catch Chester."

"I agree," Lil said. "We've already done the hard part. Gustav's a professional." She frowned. "If he's still talking to us, that is."

Juliette took Aimée's hand and squeezed. "It's okay to get help from adults sometimes."

Aimée pouted. Why did everyone see the world differently from her?

Lil and Charlotte stepped outside the cave and waited for their rescuers. Kalin snuggled up to her brother. What if this was a dream and he disappeared again?

~

Chester stood in the rack house of the distillery. How many more could he take without it being noticed? He'd do it tonight, right after shift's end, and with help from his cousin Dickie.

Frowning, he stepped outside onto the platform. He had to get that wheel going. Those giant paddles would turn all right, yet when the water pumped in, the thing would stall out. Thank the saints above, the boss was gone, left on some emergency. Chester smirked hopefully. Maybe something happened to his other kid—the daughter. That would solve things nicely and keep the boss away for a long while.

Hearing a voice call him back inside, he bit down on his unlit cigarette and shouted through gritty teeth. "Yeah, yeah, hold your horses. I'm comin'.

～

Breen pointed his flashlight ahead of them in the tunnel. "Look yonder. Girls in the cave!"

Gustav stopped and squinted down the dim hallway. Two silhouettes, slightly illuminated by wavering fire light, stood at what looked to be an opening. "Gotcha," he whispered, then said out loud, "It looks like Lil and my lady, Charlotte."

"How do you know?" Declan asked. "And where's my daughter?" He growled.

"I know because they're the tallest two. Kalin's probably inside that cave with the twins. Looks like they've built a fire." He couldn't help but admire these kids. French intelligence material, for sure. Who would suspect a bunch of young girls as spies?

"If Kalin's there, she's going to hear about it," Declan grouched. "Worrying us like this."

"I'd keep my temper in check," Gustav said. "Those girls are here for a reason. Let's find out why before you blow off steam." What Gustav didn't say was that his HSR showed six human light fields, not five. Was it too much to hope they'd found the missing Finn?

As Declan got closer, Lil said, "Hello, sir. There's someone here you'll want to see."

Declan scowled. "Oh, I'll want to do more than see her." Lil and Charlotte took each arm and walked him into the cavern. He took in the fire and his little lass sitting way too close to a beastly looking lad—a vagabond? "Holy Mary Mother in Heaven ... who in Hades are you?"

The stranger stood, shakily. "Da, it's me. Don't you recognize your own son!"

This time it was Declan whose legs gave way.

He was a large man and nearly pulled everyone down. Straightening, Declan rushed to his son and pulled him into an embrace. Mournful sobs echoed off the stone walls.

Everyone circled father and son as Finn tearfully told what had happened since his disappearance, and where to find the stolen casks.

Declan said, "Before my son disappears again, let's get the lad home."

"Right," Gustav said. "We can make a stretcher with these blankets. You and Breen carry Finn to the SUV. The girls will go with you. I'll keep these two brothers with me. We'll hike down to the casks and guard them until you come back with something to haul them off."

Lil glared at Gustav. "I'm staying here with you. Besides, I know how to set Chester up for his final undoing. Tonight." Her grin was positively wicked.

"Yes!" Aimée agreed. "We have to find the casks. It's the reason for our trip to Ireland." She had to see this through to the end, as they had promised at Madame Villars's waterfall. "Besides," she added, "We found them and found Finn."

"And excellent work it was," Gustav said earnestly. "But off you go, ladies, no arguing. "Once we get the barrels back, we'll come to the house." He bowed slightly. "*Mademoiselle*

Lil, I promise to listen to your idea. Later." He worried about who they'd find at the shore. He was more than capable of defending himself and suspected the B brothers could too. But the girls—he'd have to teach them defensive techniques, and soon.

Gustav followed the B brothers, who were familiar with the tunnel that ran to the coast. Thanks to Finn's directions, they found the missing whiskey barrels. The place was deserted, so they stood a steady guard to wait for Declan. The transfer had to be done in a way that wouldn't alert anyone. Chester was due a well-deserved shock tonight after his shift.

The men laid Finn in the back of the SUV, covering him with the same blankets he'd lived with for months. Grudgingly, Lil and Aimée climbed inside. But the other girls were happy to travel home with him. The medallion warmed slightly as Charlotte held it. It knows we found him, she thought.

As the vehicle drove away, Lil saw something familiar. "Look!" She said, pointing. Hotspur appeared in between layers of undulating fog. He was perched on top of a henge-stone. "You might be right, Aimée, about a vortex at this abbey, too." She peered around intently. Was Mother Weed watching them right now?

"That giant falcon," Finn said. "It saved my life, you know.

"What do you mean?" Lil asked.

"I don't know where it came from, but it dropped off care packages. I'd have probably met my maker by now without its help."

Kalin took her brother's arm. "Oh, Finn. We have so much to tell you."

Chapter 33

Homecoming

As the dusty black vehicle pulled up before the stone summer house, Mrs. Macready flew out the door and down the porch steps. After hours of worrying, her knowing had finally kicked in, the girls were found. She hugged each one thoroughly before noticing a beggar in the car.

"Kalin, what have you brought us now, lass?

Breen took his sister's hand. "Come closer, sister. You said ye knew he was alive."

Charlotte had helped Finn to a seated position, and he blinked hard in the light. "It takes more than an explosion to kill this Irishman."

Throwing her hands over her face, the housekeeper let out a sob. "I never believed you were dead!" She stiffened her spine, but her voice quavered. "Let's get you inside. I'll run a bath, and when you're done eating my lovely fish chowder, you'll have a nice shave."

"Brilliant," Finn said, thinking his heart might explode from joy.

∿

After Declan had delivered his son into capable hands, he called his wife with the miraculous news. He'd barely finished the sentence when she ran to her car to begin the hour-long drive to their summer home and the son she had believed dead. Declan wished he could stay, but he had the business of the stolen casks to deal with. Besides, this was exactly what Finn needed now, to be gently cared for. He didn't need his bristly old father just yet. And Declan had arrangements to make. He hoped their retrieval of the whiskey wouldn't alert the Corkys or their idiot mule, Chester.

∿

Gustav and the triplets, minus Breen, sat in the frigid cavern guarding fifty barrels of whiskey.

"We'll have our hands full loading these," the shortest B brother said, staring up at the stacks. He was the weakest triplet and worried he'd not be able to pull his weight.

"We'll be fine, monsieur," Gustav said. "There are four of us to do the lugging. Not saying it won't be a workout, but it'll get done."

"Maybe we should start rolling 'em out now," the worried brother said, shaking hair away from his face.

His brother disagreed. "No. We should wait, like. We don't want Corkys sneakin' up on us. Sister says they've been lurking about. She seen their cigarette butts down the beach."

Gustav stood and stretched, flexing his impressive biceps. "I don't worry about a few criminal blowhards."

The brothers nodded, sensing there wasn't much the intelligence man was afraid of.

They quieted, and waited and waited, then …

"Listen," Gustav said. "I hear an engine."

They trotted out of the tunnel and onto the beach, and squinted out to sea. On the horizon was a large fishing boat disappearing between cresting waves. It was headed right toward them.

~

With a deep sigh, Finn sank into hot, lavender-scented water. "Don't fall asleep in there!" Mrs. Macready yelled through the bathroom door.

"I won't!" he hollered back. But, of course, he did.

"He should get out now," Charlotte said impatiently. "He's had long enough to clean up. After all he's been through, we don't want to lose him in the tub."

"You're right, lass." Mrs. Macready turned to sounds on the steps and ran down the hall to greet Finn's mother with a long, tearful hug.

"Is he in there?—Finnegan, it's your mum, I'm coming in."

Mrs. Macready took Charlotte's arm and led her to the stairs. "He's in good hands now, dear. Let's go make tea and toast. I baked enough bread for the entire village. Nothing else to do with my worry time."

They passed the dining table where Lil and the twins sat and paced. We know who sat and who paced. "Aimée! Please sit down!" Lil said, pulling fingers away from her temples. "You're making me crazy. I'm working out the final intrigue for tonight's capture of Chester."

Aimée stopped. "You and I should hike along the beach to the caves. See what's going on. They might need our help."

Juliette pulled her sister into an oversized chair to sit with her. "Patience, remember?"

Aimée took a deep breath. "I'm trying!"

Lil snorted.

"Really. I am."

Kalin stood. "I'm going upstairs. I want to hug Finn again before he goes to sleep. He'll probably sleep for a week."

"Are you coming with us tonight to the distillery?" Aimée asked.

"And leave my brother again? Never! I trust you to bring justice to our family."

"We will!" they said together.

The afternoon passed like molasses pouring uphill. Fresh bread was toasted and eaten, and pots of tea emptied down to the dregs. Mrs. Macready tried to read the leaves but couldn't focus. Even though Finn was home, she feared the nightmare was not yet over.

When the honey bread was down to two loaves, they heard Declan's truck pull in. Chairs scratched the pine wood floor as the girls ran to the front door. Declan, Gustav, and the B brothers poured out of the oversized vehicle and tromped up the porch steps.

Declan raced in and up the stairs to greet his waiting wife. "How's our son?"

"Fine now, thank the angels. We shaved and cut that jungle hair. He's sleeping like a baby."

Declan peeked in the room to see the son he remembered, not the tunnel rat he'd turned into, poor chap. Then he looked skyward in thanks.

On the porch, Gustav turned to the triplets and shook each hand heartily, thanking them for their help. "Head on home, now, boys. We'll take care of tonight."

"But," Breen said, "we want to help, if we can."

Gustav winked a command. "We'll call if we need you." Reluctantly, the brothers left. Gustav shouted toward the kitchen, "We need coffee, Mrs. Mac. And make it triple strong. We're likely to be up all night."

Relieved to be given an important task, Mrs. Macready rushed to the kitchen.

Soon Declan joined everyone at the table and stared at Gustav, praying he had a good plan. His own mind was a swamp. "So, what next, my man?"

Gustav's own mind reeled with possibilities. "A plan to catch a rat."

Silence permeated the room.

Lil cleared her throat and stood up. "I ... I've actually got an idea." She flipped back her ebony ponytail. The exotic streak had matured her but made her look more cunning than wise. "And I'm pretty sure you'll like it," she grinned her lopsided smile. "However, someone has to drive me to the henge stones, near the abbey."

"Okay, I'll take you," Gustav said. "So long as you tell me your wicked plan along the way." Somehow, he found himself trusting her instincts.

"Absolutely, Monsieur Gustav. What are we waiting for?"

Chapter 34

Catching a Rat

Inside the distillery, the midnight bell rang marking the end of the night shift. Chester's coworkers stood in line at the time clock and punched out one by one. He lurked in the doorway of the rack house where they'd loaded new casks for maturing, deciding which barrels would be easiest to take tonight. He'd already faked an inventory list that would cover his tracks.

"I'm getting good at this," he sniggered under his breath.

"Ain't you comin'?" The last guy in line asked, waiting to turn off the lights.

"Naw. Gotta take one more look at the wheel."

"It workcd all right tonight. What's the problem then?"

"Just want to make sure. You know how the old man is."

"Yeah, I hear ya. Well, shut everything down afore you leave."

"Don't you worry," Chester said. "I'll take care of everything."

After the last man left, Chester switched off the lights and stepped outside onto the canal platform. He signaled upstream with his flashlight, one beam, two beams, then three, the usual signal to his cousin Dickie. The full moon cast a light path onto the water, illuminating Dickie who quietly paddled a sturdy skiff toward the platform. Well look at Dickie, all lit up like a saint, Chester thought. A good omen.

Dickie tied off the boat and stumbled up the ladder. "How many we got for t'night?" he asked, pushing back a thick mat of hair with greasy fingers.

Chester sniffed. "What you been eating? Your mouth is covered in greasy charcoal bits."

"I had to do something waitin' all night, didn't I?" He snorted. "If you must know, Crowley's grilled ribs and a couple of pints, is all."

Chester swatted his cousin's neck. "Told you not to drink nothin' till after."

Dickie swayed then caught himself. "I'm f ... fine," he slurred. "Let's get this o'er with. There's a girl waitin' on me at Crowleys."

Chester shook his head, then lit a cigarette and stuck it between his teeth. "One smoke is all, and then we grab the barrels."

Dickie lit up too, and together they watched the moon creep up the sky. "Did I mention? You need to start payin' me more."

Chester flicked his cigarette into the canal and watched the current pull it away in seconds. "You say that every time. Let's get 'er done."

They worked for a half hour rolling six barrels onto the skiff without dropping one into the water. "We need a heavier boat, next time, Dickie. Then we'll take more."

"You pay more. I get a bigger boat."

Like a shock wave, a man's voice came from inside the building. "Shh," Chester spit out, as his head jerked toward the sound. In the doorway stood a shadowy man. The ghostly sight sent every drop of blood to drain down Chester's body. "H ... holy saints on h ... high. It can't be. You're not real!" He shouted.

Finn approached, and stared down at the puny scoundrel, his blue eyes reflecting light from the moon. The blue eyes blinked. "I am alive, Chester. More alive than I've been in months, no thanks to you. You're a thief. And a killer."

Chester stumbled backwards, away from what was surely a mirage. Maybe this was his conscience, haunting him. "You ... you can't be. I saw you ... your boat. Dickie! Look. What I'm seein' here is a ghost. Can you see 'em?"

Then, another, deeper voice sounded, "This ghost is with me." Declan stepped out from behind his son, and pointed to Gustav standing with him. "See this man? He and I will be holding you for the police, who are on their way, right now."

Gustav, dressed like a special forces soldier, stepped into the moonlight. Now Chester realized the game was up. He'd never make it by all three men, especially not this one.

A motor started. "Get in the boat," Dickie yelled. "We'll escape to the river."

Chester spun around and ran toward the boat, slipping and falling onto the wet platform. Legs and arms flailing, he spider-crawled toward the boat. Dickie bungled up the ladder to help, but missed his step and fell into the skiff with a thud.

As Chester pulled himself up, a terrifying screech pierced the night sky. He craned his neck to see a monster-bird flying toward him at full speed. It looked like something from the dinosaur age. A dragon from hell come to get him, he thought, and turned to run. But the winged creature kept coming and bumped a shoulder, knocking him off balance. Chester's arms flew into the air, then pinwheeled like a slow-motion cartoon, propelling his body backwards into the canal, where it made a loud splash.

As if waiting for this very moment, the water-wheel turned on with a loud, scraping sound as a wide wooden panel grabbed Chester's shirt sleeve. The panel dragged him deep into the briny water of the canal. Every man present watched Chester disappear into the watery channels of justice.

Sirens sounded in the distance.

Chapter 35

Heading Home

Two days later, after a much-needed rest for everyone, Declan drove Gustav and the girls to the Dublin airport. Once there, the girls and their bodyguard would fly directly to Lyon, France, where the twins' parents would meet them for the trip back to school.

"I booked you in first-class," Declan said. "A gift from me and the missus, and it's the least we can do. We're beholden to you, especially you lasses, for finding our boy and helping our Kalin." His face held a mixture of joy and melancholy.

Gustav turned to the detective team and offered a smile. It wasn't a smile, really, but a quick nod where one corner of his lips turned up slightly. Coming from their usually serious guardian, bodyguard, intelligence man, the girls took this as high approval. "It's strange to see you foursome sitting back there without the little redhead." He turned back to Declan. "But we understand her wanting to stay home."

Declan nodded. "The missus and I can't bear to have either of our kids away right now. And Kalin has become inseparable from that rascal, Shamrock. Even Finn's taken to 'em."

"Thank God for that," Lil said, delighted not to be putting up with the gregarious pooch anymore. "By the way, Mr. Declan, when you were at the police station, did they say anything more about the body?"

"They said Chester's body was long gone, swept down to the river and out to sea. He may never leave that wild sea of ours, or he could be on the way to Greenland by now. But that idiot Dickie is behind bars. He'll not be thievin' on anybody for a long while."

"Maybe Chester was lunch for sharks," Lil said, not afraid to picture it.

"That would be poetic justice now, wouldn't it?" Gustav agreed.

Juliette leaned forward. "Our papa is a fan of poetic justice, right Aimée?" Although she didn't fully understand what it meant, she knew the Universe had a way of righting a wrong.

"*Oui*, a big fan," Aimée said. "And we had examples of that last semester, didn't we?"

Glumly, Charlotte stared out the window. Yes, last semester. And now, another mystery solved by the detective team. But she missed Kalin and Finn already. Is this how it went? You made friends then lost friends? Not her experience growing up in the stuffy home of a duke.

Juliette touched her arm. "Are you okay?"

"I'll be fine. Post-drama depression, I guess." She clung to the medallion and smiled weakly.

"Once we're back at school," Juliette went on, "you'll be too busy to miss them. Plus, you can ride your horse." At the thought of Bolt, Charlotte perked up.

"And we'll see Danni!" Lil said. "He's been texting like crazy. I'm calling him as soon as we get close to Dublin." Her phone pinged. "It's Danni," she cried, putting the call on speaker.

"Can't wait to see everybody," Danni said. "And I have two surprises."

"What surprises?" Aimée asked.

"I'm coming with you, on the drive back to school. And my hair."

"What's with your hair?" Aimée asked,

"You'll have to wait to find out," he said mysteriously. "Can't wait to see you guys. Gotta go. Chef Marie just pulled chocolate filled muffins from the oven." The line went dead.

~

The shuffle through the airport was typically chaotic, but soon they were all seated in first-class, pampered by flight attendants bringing them juice and cookies. And something stronger for Gustav. Soon the jet soared up through thick clouds breaking free into a deep blue sky, as they settled in for the two-and-a-half-hour flight.

After the slog through French customs, they made it to the receiving area to see Danni and the twins' parents waiting. The girls talked all at once, forcing Danni to cover his ears. Abruptly they stopped and stared at his hair, realizing it now sported two purple streaks. He smiled, showing the cute space between his front teeth. "Well, what do you think?" he asked shyly, his lisp more prominent.

"It looks incredible," Lil said before turning a shade of pink. Danni blushed, too.

The twins' papa removed his arms from around his girls. "Come along, everyone. Charlotte, your parents sent their limousine for Gustav to drive us all to school. They said they'd see you on the next break. The car's right out front."

Charlotte was fine not seeing her parents just yet. This was her family now, people who understood her and who were capable of showing their love. She smiled warmly.

Soon everyone was tucked inside the sleek black car, Danni between Lil and Charlotte, faced the twins and their parents.

Gustav looked down to see his manor house driver's cap waiting on the passenger seat. He put it on and easily slid back into his chauffeur role. "Ready? We're off to the Abbey."

～

The long drive went by in a flash. The girls entertained Danni and the twins' parents with a rundown of all that had happened on their adventure. The adults exchanged strangled looks with Gustav in the rearview mirror, but no details came forth about the dangers, now thankfully behind them.

"We're relieved," said the twins' papa. "Now you'll be safe at the Abbey. Ah look, there it is." He pointed out the window at the stone mansion on the hill.

Lil shouted. "Wait! Something's different."

Aimée put her nose to the window. "You're right. It doesn't look the same at all. And we didn't pass through the vortex!"

"And look," Juliette said. "That sign says it's a museum."

"What vortex?" Celeste said.

"Later, Maman," Juliette said.

Confusion and silence prevailed as Gustav drove closer to the building, now looking noticeably different. A large, paved parking lot sat adjacent to the stone estate. The portico was still out front, but freshly painted as were all the window frames. They watched people go in and out of the heavy wooden doors, dressed in modern-day clothes.

"Where's the horse barn?" Charlotte asked. And internally cried, Where's Bolt?

Gustav pulled into an empty space and had barely stopped when the girls dove out of the car and raced to the front door of the school—or former school—now a museum.

"What? What is going on?" Aimée cried. They stared at the same—but not the same—Abbey.

"We never went back in time," Lil said. "This is the Abbey now, in our own century."

Just then, they heard a familiar shriek and looked up to see Hotspur soaring over the crumbling stone tower in the near distance. He held something in his mouth.

They ran, trailed by Danni, to a tall pile of rocks near the tower, surrounded by foliage at the base. Hearing a plop, Lil crashed through shrubbery toward something wrapped around a rock. She opened a linen cloth with words on it. "It's a note. I'll read it."

> Dearest ladies,
>
> Mother Weed has closed the vortex. Not because we do not wish to see you. We miss you terribly. But the Abbey is in peril, too perilous for your return. Do you remember when Keeper said I can be a warrior when I have to be? Well, dear ones, that time is now. When it's safe to return, we will send a sign. In the meantime, don't worry; we have faced these enemies before. I hope the wait is not too long before we see you again. And congratulations on solving Kalin's mysterious haunting. We always believed you could do it.
>
> Yours with love,
> The Abbess

The girls glared in shock; Lil's face more pale than usual. "I bet they're under attack—maybe from the Ottomans. That's happened before. Apparently."

"The who?" Charlotte asked.

Danni piped in. "Do you mean warriors from the Ottoman Empire? They did try to take over France once, and other countries too. I remember learning about it in school: "a time of great unrest,'" he quoted from memory.

Aimée threw up her hands. "What do we do now?"

Danni watched the giant bird soar away, giving off a good-bye shriek. "Let's go back to the inn. Madame Villars will know, and maybe will show us what's happening in her waterfall."

"Good idea," Lil said. "If the Abbey is under attack, we have to figure out a way to help. We can't let anything bad happen to them!"

Gustav strolled up to the group. "Is the vortex closed?"

"What?" Lil asked. "You know about the time-line vortex?"

"What kind of intelligence officer would I be if I hadn't figured it out?"

Lil grinned. "Well then, take us to the inn. Looks like we have another mystery to solve."

The End

The Haunting of the Irish Girl

Acknowledgements

They say writing and publishing the next books is "easier" than the first. But authors of all levels of experience need helpers. I'm lucky to have a husband who has unlimited patience with my daily writing, my unpredictable daydreaming, and my middle-of-the-night bursts of vision. Thank you, sweetie. Thanks to members of my writers' group for falling in love with these characters and the story, and for your gentle critiques and ideas that enlivened the adventure. I'm also grateful to friend and artist, Maury Kettell, for giving the story atmosphere with his illustrations. And to my designer, John Bragg, an author himself, I couldn't have done it without your technical expertise that actually put the physical book into the hands of readers.

About the Author

Judi Valentine grew up hiking and exploring the dense woods and granite mountains of the great state of Maine. She was always scribbling about something, and when unforgettable adventures of magical realism popped into her mind's eye, she decided to pen them into stories. For the last five years, she has written fiction for young readers and crime stories. *The Haunting of the Irish Girl* is her third novel and the second book of this series. Over the years, Judi has had short stories and articles published in regional publications in Maine and Maryland. In March of 2017, she published her first novel for young readers, *The Crystal Chain,* and in 2019 *The Reluctant Ghost of Brivalle Castle,* both available at www.jvalentinebooks.com, and on Amazon. In 2003, during her career as a PhD nutritionist, Judi co-authored and published a high-selling workbook on diet and nutrition.

Made in the USA
Columbia, SC
21 August 2021